AMBUSHED!

Raider kept watching the hut, expecting the commotion in the corral to bring Dog Ruben out of the hut. But the horses settled down again before anyone took notice.

"Time to go get 'im," Raider said aloud.

He stood up, but then lurched backward away from the corral. The man had come out of the horses, working his way through the herd to vault over the top of the corral.

He was flying straight toward Raider, his knife drawn, his face twisted in a horrible scowl . . .

Other books in the RAIDER series by
J. D. HARDIN

RAIDER
SIXGUN CIRCUS
THE YUMA ROUNDUP
THE GUNS OF EL DORADO
THIRST FOR VENGEANCE
DEATH'S DEAL
VENGEANCE RIDE
CHEYENNE FRAUD
THE GULF PIRATES
TIMBER WAR
SILVER CITY AMBUSH
THE NORTHWEST RAILROAD WAR
THE MADMAN'S BLADE
WOLF CREEK FEUD
BAJA DIABLO
STAGECOACH RANSOM
RIVERBOAT GOLD
WILDERNESS MANHUNT
SINS OF THE GUNSLINGER
BLACK HILLS TRACKDOWN

GUNFIGHTER'S SHOWDOWN

B

BERKLEY BOOKS, NEW YORK

GUNFIGHTER'S SHOWDOWN

A Berkley Book/published by arrangement with
the author

PRINTING HISTORY
Berkley edition/March 1989

For information address: The Berkley Publishing Group,
200 Madison Avenue, New York, NY 10016.

ISBN: 0-425-11461-9

A BERKLEY BOOK ® TM 757,375
Berkley Books are published by the Berkley Publishing Group,
200 Madison Avenue, New York, NY 10016

PRINTED IN THE UNITED STATES OF AMERICA

10 9 8 7 6 5 4 3 2 1

This book is dedicated to the following people:
Bob and Carol Eldred
George Francois
Butch Francois
Richard LaBrecque
Stanley Edelman
Debra Cartwright
and Cubby

ONE

Raider was driving hard for Nogales, Arizona, when the bay mare stepped in a hole and broke her leg. She staggered a few steps before she crumpled to the ground. Raider managed to swing his left leg over as the mare fell sideways onto the dusty plain. His right leg wasn't as lucky, remaining in the stirrup when he tried to roll away from the struggling mount. The hard plain stopped his backside, knocking the air from his lungs.

For a second, he flashed the thoughts he had experienced many times before—the ultimate surge of fear that surely was the prelude to death. His chest burned inside his thick cotton shirt; there was a sharp stabbing in his lower back. He sucked for air, but nothing worked in his guts.

Killed by a falling horse, thought the big Pinkerton agent from Arkansas. And all the time he had figured Dog Ruben and the horse thieves would get him.

"What a stupid goddam way to die!"

He heard himself say it.

He heard himself wheezing in the first breath.

His eyes focused and the blue expanse of the Arizona sky loomed over him. At first he wondered if he might be dead but then he realized that for now he was probably going to live and let Dog Ruben have a chance at killing him.

Why did they call him Dog Ruben? That seemed a strange name for a Mexican horse thief. Not Ruben, necessarily, but the Dog part was unusual.

Some said he liked to eat dog, which was not that unusual. Indians and Mexicans both like to stew a dog now and then, and Raider himself had eaten it on a couple of occasions, although he would never admit it, even in the roughest company. Dog didn't taste bad when you were really hungry.

His black eyes rolled around in his head. Why was he thinking like that? The fall had dazed him. And he didn't want to think about the pain in his ankle, the one that was still caught in the stirrup.

But he had to sit up, so he tried. His brain spun for a while, but he gradually focused on his leg. He started to reach up to untangle his foot, but the mare struggled again, trying to rise.

Raider drew his Colt .45 Peacemaker from his holster, thumbing the hammer to put the animal out of its misery. He hesitated when the mare raised her head and looked pitifully at him. When she put her head down again, Raider wanted to cry.

He flopped back on the ground, lying there like a fool. He'd never catch Dog Ruben now. That sly Mexican bastard, slipping up into the Arizona horse country to filch a couple of nice remudas. Raider figured he only had three or four men working with him. Nothing too big for the Pinkerton's '76 Winchester. Not if he got the drop on them.

Considering his foe, Raider built up new energy. The ranchers had hired the agency to stop Dog Ruben and his men. If Raider didn't come through on the assignment, Allan Pinkerton and William Wagner would think he was getting old. He also spotted a buzzard circling overhead, which imbued him with a strong will to survive.

He sat up again. The mare lay still, allowing him to reach for the heel of his Justin boot. The boot wouldn't come out of the stirrup, but he was able to dislodge his foot from the boot and stand up on the tender ankle. His rugged face twisted in a grimace as he limped around. If it was broken, he would never get off the plain alive.

Raider wheeled on his good leg, aiming his gun and firing down at the bay. She shivered and her tongue lolled out. Gone. He wanted to cry again. Not for the mare, but for himself. But he didn't cry, mainly because it seemed like a waste of time, something he had precious little of.

"Might as well rest my bones," he muttered.

He sat on the back haunch of the mare, taking stock.

Pains: ankle and back hurting. Mount: none. Guns: Colt ready, Winchester under the dead mare, have to get it out. Hat: Lying in the dust. Other boot: Still tangled in the stirrup. Chances: Bad—buzzard bad.

He dusted off his blue jeans and leather vest. It hadn't been long since his last bath and shave, but he felt like a hot tub would perk him up. He had to settle for the canteen on his saddle. At least the canteen wasn't under the mare. He drank a couple of swallows and rubbed his face with a handful of the lukewarm liquid.

Raider turned to look south over the wavy heat lines of the sweltering plain. He had been so close to Dog Ruben. The trail was clear and fresh. And him without a mount. Raider had to laugh. Working for the horse ranchers and he didn't even have a horse.

How long had he been riding the bay? He couldn't remember. She had been a good one. He felt bad about having to shoot her.

"Damn it all."

The sun was frying the top of his head, scrambling his disappointments even more. He stood again, absently applying pressure to the tender ankle. It twinged for a second but then eased off a little as he started to walk. He was able to pick up his black Stetson and shield his head from the killer sun. Then he untangled his boot and slid it on over the swollen ankle.

Nothing to do but wait for evening and try to walk it. In the meantime, he could try to get his saddle off the mare. He could use it for shade, with the saddle blanket. Wouldn't be a bad idea to have his Winchester in hand either. A man never knew when he was liable to come across greater numbers who would take advantage of their strength to extract a profit from an unfortunate soul.

He worked the rest of the hot afternoon, grunting and groaning, wrestling with the saddle until it finally came loose. Luckily the rifle scabbard came with it, freeing his '76. At least he could plug a rabbit or a prairie hen, roast it over a fire. If he had time.

Time for what? he asked himself. To catch Dog Ruben? Walking?

He slung the saddle over his shoulder and started south.

How the hell was he going to get Dog Ruben? The thief was probably almost to the Mexican border by now. When he took the stolen horse herd over the border, Raider could no longer follow him, legally anyway. Of course, legality was always open for interpretation and borders weren't exactly drawn across the land like they were on a map.

How the hell was he going to make it to the border? Walking?

He told himself to shut up and not to panic. He had been in a lot of stewpots in his travels for Mr. Pinkerton. He had to laugh. Like a dog in a stewpot. Dog Ruben.

"Damn it all!"

His tired legs carried him forward with a limping gait. The ankle ached with a dull pain now, not nearly as bad as it had been. Sometimes if you walked on an injury, it got better right away. Maybe he was finally going to get lucky. A man in his line of work often relied on good fortune.

But this time it was going to be served up bad. He felt the cooler air as the sun disappeared behind him. He turned to look back at the thunderhead growing over the plain. Where the hell had it come from? It never rained this far south. Not much anyway.

He shook his head when he saw something else in the sky. "You just ain't gonna leave me alone, are you?"

Soaring the currents that preceded the storm was the black dot of a buzzard that hopefully followed the big man's limping southward trek.

The storm came quickly from the north, boiling down with dark vapors and thunderous rain. His saddle kept some of the water off him, but he was still drenched by the time the cloudburst subsided. Rolling southward, the storm made a hasty departure, returning the sun to make steam from the puddles almost before they could seep into the dry ground. Raider kept walking through the whole thing, figuring to stay with it as long as his ankle held out. If he stopped, it might stiffen up on him, so it was best to keep moving, if only to get closer to Nogales.

How far was he? A man had said a two-day ride, but that had been three days ago. Of course, the Mexicans had not taken a straight trail south, which had kept him wandering back and forth across the plain. Maybe Nogales was just ahead, on the blank horizon.

What was it his old Uncle Coleman used to say? Drink deep, ride hard, and don't look too far over the horizon.

Raider thought that was the stupidest thing he had ever heard.

Maybe he wasn't even walking toward Nogales.

At least the sun was falling, although the heat was still with him at dusk. Nights on the plain could be as cold as winter in Calgary. He didn't have his shearling coat with him. Only the wet saddle blanket.

The buzzard dipped a little lower in an arc over the reddening horizon to the west. On Raider's right. He was heading south. There'd have to be horses in Nogales.

He'd never catch Dog Ruben Mijares. Not walking with a saddle on his shoulder. Not with an injured ankle.

His miseries would have been dealt with accordingly, only the bugs decided to rise up out of the sage and greasewood. They swarmed around him in the half-light of sunset, biting and flying into his eyes. It felt like they were going to descend on him and eat him alive, chewing the meat right off his bones, but then, through the wall of insects, Raider saw the trail of smoke from a wood fire.

Raider fought the urge to run toward the bump on the dimming horizon. The bump became a shape and then a slapdash hovel with a crude corral behind it. Raider approached cautiously, his hand hanging low by the redwood handle of his Peacemaker. He held the saddle on his left shoulder, so he could use it like a shield if someone started firing on him.

The house was made of scrap wood and adobe bricks. No light, except the flickering of the fire. No movement. Raider started toward the door. He figured to knock until he heard the chortling of a rifle lever.

A high voice told him in Spanish not to come any closer.

Raider looked up to the roof of the house. A Mexican man stood on the wooden rows of scrap lumber. He was aiming an old Henry rifle at Raider's chest. The end of the rifle was trembling, the bore a nervous black eye.

"I don't want t' kill you," Raider said. "I just want t' rest a spell. Let me be and nobody gets hurt."

"But you are the wan who will be hurt, gringo! Drop the saddle an' stand where I can see you."

Raider figured the man couldn't hit anything with his hands shaking so badly. So Raider moved, his aches and pains now gone in the excitement of the challenge. His body came to life, lean sinews reacting to the threat without much thought.

He shuffled the saddle in front of him, dropping it to the ground. In the moment that he was shielded from the rifle, he reached for the Colt on his hip. As the saddle fell, he came up firing.

The Mexican gaped at the quickness of Raider's sleight of hand. His finger tightened on the rifle trigger, but he never got the chance to fire. Raider's Colt kicked up splinters at his feet, throwing him off balance. He teetered for an instant and then tripped backward, crashing through the thin roof of the hovel.

Raider heard him hit and cry out inside.

The big man sighed. "I told 'im I didn't want any trouble."

"All right, señor!" the man cried from the house. "You ween. Just come een here an' help me."

As Raider started cautiously toward the front door, he caught sight of the corral. One grey gelding, half-swaybacked and broken down, stood languidly by a water trough. Not a horse to catch Dog Ruben on, even if the Mexican decided to sell it to him.

"Señor, help me!"

Raider eased into the doorway, which was covered only by a tattered cloth. He expected an ambush from his ungracious host, but instead he saw a defeated man squirming on the bed of coals from the fire. Raider grabbed the Mexican and pulled him out of the house, dropping him in a sticky puddle. The man's backside sizzled in the mud.

"I hates thees damn terr'tory," the Mexican said. "If I have any people leff een Meh-hee-koh, I go back there pronto."

Raider shrugged. "I didn't want t' mix it up, Pedro."

"I am Rodrigo!" the man cried indignantly. "And I curse thees terr'tory from thee first day here."

"Yeah, me too."

Rodrigo suddenly looked up at the big man. "Señor, you shoots so you do not keel me. You must be a *pistolero*. I thank you for not keeling me. I thought you were riding weeth thee Dog."

Raider's eyes narrowed. "What do you know about Dog Ruben?" He aimed his Colt at the man's hapless face. "Let's have it, Rigo."

"I knew eet!" Rodrigo cried. "You are wan of thee Dog men!"

"I ain't," the big man insisted.

The Mexican's eyes were wide. "Then why you hold your *pistola* to keel me?"

Raider eased off with the Peacemaker, keeping it ready by his side. "All right, no gun. What do you know about the Dog man?"

"I tell you thees," Rodrigo cried with his finger in the air. "He ees called Dog because he has thee face of thee dog. He is Ruben Mee-har-rays. I curse heem an' all hees people."

"That ain't enough," Raider replied. "You seen 'im lately?"

Rodrigo gazed into the black irises of the tall stranger. "Tell me who you are, gringo."

"Pinkerton agent. Been hired by the horse ranchers round Tucson t' bring in this Dog Ruben. He's stealin' ever'body blind."

"Ha!" the man said with another punctuating gesture. "He was here not two hours before you. Steal every damn horse I have, except thee grey. He would not even take eet to eat eet."

Raider shook his head. "Bastards. What'd they do? Just ride in 'nd take ever'thin'?"

Rodrigo nodded. "*Sí*, señor."

"Lucky they didn't cut your throat," the big man offered.

The Mexican touched his throat with his fingers. "They don't keel me only because I am one of their people."

"Did they seem t' know I'm after 'em?"

Rodrigo shrugged. "I do not know. They come, they went. They let me leeve. What else should I care? I have no horses now."

Raider helped the man out of the mud. "Tell you what, Rigo. You help me out an' I'll get your horses back."

"Why for should Dog Ruben need my horses?" Rodrigo asked to the darkening heavens. "He have so many."

"How many head you think?" Raider asked.

"Ah . . . maybe a hundred."

"Four men with 'im?"

Rodrigo gaped at the big man. "Sí. How you know thees?"

Raider waved it off. "Look here, Rigo. I gotta ride. I want that nag, if that's all you got."

Rodrigo suddenly jumped into the foray, becoming a horse trader. "Thee joke ees on thee Dog, señor. He take all thee horses but leave Rodrigo thee fastes' one. I have thee saddle for eet, too. Thee Dog did not want my saddles."

Raider looked skeptically at the nag. "Shit. How much you want for it?"

"The horse ees nothing. You can have eet to chase thee Dog. But for the saddle you must pay . . . say . . . twelve American dollar."

Raider reached into his pocket. "I got a saddle. Here's two bucks. If you want another eight for the nag when I get back, I'll see that you get it somehow. Otherwise you gotta trust me for the rest."

Rodrigo took the two dollars. "Sí, señor. Ees better trade than I get from thee Dog."

"Some food," Raider continued, "Beans, whatever you got."

"Sí, if you weel bring back my horses."

"I'll sure as hell try, Rigo."

Raider felt a twinge of pain in his ankle. He wanted to soak it in hot water, but he only had time to wrap it. The pain didn't matter anymore. Dog Ruben Mijares was only two hours in front of him and the urge to catch the horse thief was a lot stronger than the aching in his leg.

see nothing to indicate that Dog Ruben's men had brought the stolen remuda this way.

Maybe they had come down another route, swinging in a wider arc around Nogales. Or maybe Raider hadn't even found the St. Miguel River. Maybe he was somewhere else.

Nothing to do but continue along the riverbank for a while, and see what was up ahead. It was a narrow, spring-fed little stream, winding through high sandstone knees that rose in sporadic groupings on the sinuous bank. Raider just kept on, finding his way much more easily as the sun peeked over the eastern horizon. No sign of horses. Where the hell was he?

After another quarter mile of following the streambed, the grey began to snort. It danced and tossed its head against the restraining reins. Raider patted its neck. He wondered what was bothering the grey until he caught the unmistakable scent of horses—a lot of them—corralled somewhere close by.

He tied the grey to a rock and proceeded on foot, with his Winchester in hand.

Climbing up on one of the sandstone knees, he peered around the next bend of the river. Even in the first light, he could see the horses. Dog Ruben had them penned up in a natural depression in the sandstone. Maybe a hundred head.

Beyond the corrals, upwind, sat the adobe hut where the men undoubtedly slept. A pistolero was on guard duty, although he was fast asleep, too secure in his own territory. The whole camp was quiet until Dog Ruben rode in.

The outlaw pounded in from the east with a woman clutching the cantle of his saddle and riding behind him. Judging from the fight she gave when the Dog man pulled her off, she had not come voluntarily. He dragged her inside the adobe hut, shooing out three of his sleeping men in the process.

Dog Ruben's men watched at the windows of the adobe hut until they were tired of their leader's spectacle. Then three of them went to find other sleeping places, while the guard went straight back to sleep in his chair outside the hut. They sure as hell weren't expecting a big Pinkerton first thing in the morning.

Raider eased down from the crest of the sandstone formation. He leaned back, trying to remember the last time he had slept. He took a deep breath of the morning air. He wasn't tired or hungry. He just felt like getting the whole thing over with.

When was the last time he had loaded his Winchester? He tried to slip another cartridge into the '76, but found that it was full. The sixth chamber in his Colt was also ready. His damned head wasn't clear at all.

Maybe he did need sleep.

No, he told himself, it was time to move, get it over with. He wouldn't be able to sleep until it was finished. He slid around the rocks and started moving low on the riverbank, stalking the camp in the purple glow of daybreak.

There was a shed adjacent to the corral, a tin-roofed shanty used for storage of hay and fodder. Dog Ruben wanted his horses healthy. The hay shed was better constructed than the adobe hut. It was also stacked high with bales of straw and bags of oats.

Raider could see everything as he hurried toward the edge of the corral. His black eyes flickered back and forth between the guard and the hay shed. He was sure the three men had gone to sleep under the tin roof, since it was the only shelter other than the adobe hut.

Hunkering by the wooden posts of the corral, he gulped air to catch his breath. His heart was pounding. He closed his eyes and tried to make it stop. Gradually he relaxed, or at least as much as he could with what lay ahead of him.

The horses spooked a little with Raider squatting beside them. He held his breath as a big roan stallion moved through the herd to take a look at him. The stallion looked him over, snorted, and then turned away, putting the mares and geldings at ease.

Raider rose up to see if anyone had noticed the stallion's behavior.

"Shit."

He dropped back down. The Mexican on guard in front of the adobe had awakened to peer toward the corral. Raider thumbed the hammer of the Winchester, anticipating the approach of the sentry. He hadn't wanted to shoot it out like this, but now he'd have to make the best of things.

A rooster crowed somewhere.

Raider sucked air into his burning lungs.

He'd have to plug the watchman and then shoot hell out of the others. What a pity. He had wanted to see Dog Ruben at the end of a rope.

The horses were calm.

The rooster crowed again.

A rifle exploded in the morning.

No more crowing from the rooster.

Raider eased up, looking at the hut. Suddenly two men were there. The naked one had to be Dog Ruben. He was cursing the sentry in Spanish. The shot had disturbed his fun with the reluctant lady.

The sentry explained that he had shot the rooster because he was tired of hearing it crow. And it was upsetting the horses. Dog Ruben seemed to buy the explanation, so he bellowed a warning and went back into the adobe hut. Raider could have sworn that he heard a woman cry out.

He leaned against the corral, waiting a second for things to settle. Maybe he'd let the woman exact her revenge after he caught the Dog man. Raider never could cotton to taking something that wasn't offered willingly, although men like Mijares never got it any other way.

The Dog man would have some hell to pay.

He looked back toward the hay shed. It was quiet. No movement. He started the long way around, following the arc of the corral until he could look straight up on the back of the hay shed.

Two of Dog Ruben's riders were snoring on top of the straw bales. Raider could see the tops of their heads. If he could find a way to take them without making any noise, he would only have three more to face. That might not be too bad, even in a straight-on fight.

But first he had to take them out.

He leaned the Winchester against the corral. It had to be fast. Just hit them before they knew what was happening.

If he had a rope . . .

But there wasn't one.

Damn. It might just be easier to start shooting. Let everyone get in on it. Dog Ruben would probably like that.

He peered toward the sleeping men. Their heads looked like dark melons resting on the hay. Maybe a fence post would do the trick. Slam it hard into their skulls. Of course, that would probably kill both of them, because Raider would be tempted to hit too hard rather than too soft. He hated the idea of killing them in their sleep. Live men had a chance, but a sleeping fool was at an unfair disadvantage. It was all right to capture a man while he was out, but not to kill him.

The horses spooked again behind him.

Raider wheeled to see a bobbing sombrero as it seemed to float over the backs of the stolen horses.

He hunkered again, watching the guard who had been asleep. He was coming from the spot where Raider had just been. As he rounded the curve of the corral, Raider could see the red and orange rooster hanging from his hand. He had come out to get the bird, probably to stew it up.

"Must be low on dogs," Raider muttered.

He reached into his boot, grabbing the handle of the hunting knife that always rested safely by his leg.

Funny, he thought, the ankle had stopped hurting. Or at least he had stopped noticing the pain. In fact, he thought he was feeling fine for a change.

The guard was coming to wake up one of the others, probably the cook.

Raider felt his own hunger as he turned the knife in his hands, grasping the shiny blade.

When the Mexican saw him crouched low by the horses, he dropped the rooster and started to raise his rifle.

Raider drew back and hurled the knife at the sentry's chest. It struck hard, sinking deep in the man's flesh. The guard dropped his rifle, clutching at the blade. Blood gushed between his fingers as he fell. He tried to cry out but he had no voice.

Raider knew he had to move now. He ran for the hay shed, leaping up to grab two heads of thick hair. Pulling both men off the hay, crashing with them to the ground, stunning them awake.

He kicked one of them in the head, knocking him cold.

The other one jumped him, landing on his back. Raider dipped a shoulder, flipping his attacker over onto the other body. Raider kicked again but this time he missed and the man was back up again.

He was going to shout.

Raider leaped for him, grabbing his throat, shutting off the desperate cry for help.

The man's eyes bugged out until they closed.

Raider let go of him, dropping him on top of his *compañero*. He wasn't dead, just sleeping. That was funny, waking them to put them out again. Maybe he should have gone after the Dog man first.

Tie them up, he told himself. He kept low again, stealing into the hay shed to look for rope. It was almost full morning now and he could see more easily. Where the hell was the other one? he wondered. He had taken out three of the five. One more left besides the Dog man. But he sure as hell didn't seem to be sleeping in the shed. It was empty except for a couple of roosters that were smart enough to keep from crowing.

Rope was hanging on one of the posts inside. Raider had to get his knife out of the guard's chest so he could cut off lengths to lash the two sleeping men's hands and legs. He also had to gag them in case they woke up. Hell, killing them would have been a whole lot easier. Sometimes his superstitions just plain got in the way.

When both men were tied securely, he dragged them behind the corral and put them next to their dead cohort.

Raider went back to his Winchester, pausing to listen for sounds of the third man, or see any other signs of movement. He wondered how quiet he had been with his own action. You never knew which sounds would carry in the still air of the morning.

A few of the horses shuddered in the corral.

The big stallion was moving.

Raider looked over the herd, expecting to see Dog Ruben or the other man coming for him. But there was no one, only the stallion strutting through the mares. Probably ready to start the foaling season. Raider knew just how he felt.

But he had other things to take care of.

The big man glanced up toward the sky. A grey cloud was rolling over the sun. A heavy rain might help. He could move around a lot easier.

But in spite of his waiting, no rain came.

So what next? Just go in there and get Dog Ruben? Or hunt

down the last man? He knew where Ruben was and the other man might run when his boss was caught.

The horses moved restlessly. Now the big roan was rearing, his front hooves pawing the air. Raider wondered if a coyote or a puma had been brave enough to come in and challenge the remuda in search of a meal. The big roan would probably make a coyote or a cat pay for such a stupid mistake.

Raider kept watching the hut, expecting the commotion in the corral to bring Dog Ruben out of the hut. But the horses settled down again before anyone took notice.

"Time to go get 'im," Raider said aloud.

He stood up, but then lurched backward away from the corral.

The man had come out of the horses, working his way through the herd to vault over the top of the corral.

He was flying straight toward Raider, his knife drawn, his face twisted in a horrible scowl. . . .

THREE

Allan Pinkerton and William Wagner had been up all night going over the books for the Pinkerton National Detective Agency. It was not a final reckoning, only a midyear tally demanded by Pinkerton himself. In addition to the financial records, Pinkerton and Wagner were also examining material from newspapers, magazines, and firsthand reports in an attempt to evaluate the reputation of the agency.

Image, Wagner claimed, was just as important as performance.

Making a profit also had its place, Pinkerton replied.

As morning dimmed the lamplights of Fifth Avenue in Chicago, both men were close to achieving their goals.

"Net profit in the thousands," Wagner said, peering down through his spectacles at the figure he had written at the bottom of a ledger page. He showed the number to Pinkerton as if he were almost afraid to speak it, lest it not come true. "Nearly as much as for all of last year."

The large, bearded Scotsman nodded approvingly. "Aye. We'll double this year."

Wagner took off his glasses, wiping them with a well-worn handkerchief. "Of course, there are other matters to consider."

Pinkerton sighed. "And I suppose you'll have to tell me all about this foolishness."

"Public opinion isn't foolishness, sir. We . . ."

"We're providin' men for whatever they're needed for," Pinkerton said. "Good men. Railroad guards, bank watchmen, detectives, men for personal and company protection. We've stayed out of politics and elections."

Wagner fitted his eyeglasses back on the bridge of his aristocratic nose. "I am fully aware of all that, sir." He lifted a newspaper that sat in front of him. "But we can't ignore this."

Pinkerton eyed the banner headline he had seen before: *Pinks Raid Helpless Grandmother*. Then, below the banner: "Burn her house to ground and leave her homeless."

Pinkerton waved off the headline. "Weren't our men found innocent in a court of law?"

Wagner nodded. "But that doesn't change the view of our agency in some people's minds."

"That old woman was hiding three known rustlers and killers in her barn. She fired on the Sheriff as well as our men. And to top all that, she was running a bordello and a gambling hall in her house, which was not burned down until after she was in custody, and only then by someone unknown."

"I suppose so," Wagner said. "Still, in some of the more remote locations, the populace sees their home-folk criminals as part of the local color. Things just went a bit too far when this woman took in three wanted murderers."

Pinkerton shook his head. "I can't let it bother me, William. We've got too much work to do." He sighed. "Darn it all, Raider wasn't even involved in that business with the old woman."

Wagner smirked a little. "The whole thing does sort of have his imprint on it. I daresay he would have approved of the way the case was wrapped up."

Pinkerton looked back down at his desk. "As much as I hate to admit it, William, Raider made money for us this year. He was in service double the time of most our men. It's just that . . ."

"That image?" Wagner said triumphantly.

Pinkerton wanted to protest, but he couldn't deny it.

"That's what I was talking about," Wagner went on. "Raider's particular brand of brutality may not serve this agency some day."

"We've discussed that before," Pinkerton interrupted. "There's no need to hash it over now. Some jobs just call for Raider's expertise. Although I do admit I will feel a bit relieved when he retires."

"Or when he's killed."

Pinkerton leaned back in his leather chair. "Where is Raider now?"

Wagner could not rightly remember, so he had to shuffle through some papers before he could pin down the big man from Arkansas. "Ah, here it is. He's chasing horse rustlers in Arizona. I have a wire from him dated two weeks ago. He should be on it by now."

"A gang of rustlers?" Pinkerton asked dubiously.

Wagner nodded. "Operating in a wide radius around the Tucson area. Rumored to be some Mexican bandit who isn't afraid to cross the border."

Pinkerton seemed concerned. "Should have sent some men with him."

Wagner shrugged. "You know that Raider wants to work alone, sir. He won't partner with anyone since Doc Weatherbee left the service."

Pinkerton folded his hands over his stomach. "I run this agency, William. If I say Raider works with a partner, he has to work with a partner."

Wagner's smile was a bit too much, but he said anyway: "Well, I'll be happy to relay that message to Raider any time you want me to."

His boss shot back an indignant look. "Did that ruffian file his last report?"

"Well, what there is of it," Wagner said. He picked up a crumpled scrap of paper from the desk. "Shall I read it?"

Pinkerton nodded.

Wagner lifted the grimy paper into the light. "There was some real bad men robbin' payrolls from the mines so I had to kill them to make them quit."

"That's it?" Pinkerton asked.

"As far as I know, sir. Except, of course, these letters from the president of the Colorado Mining and Ore Company, expressing his satisfaction with the way Raider dispatched the payroll thieves."

"Well, what about the case Raider had before that one?"

Wagner sifted through some papers. "No report, just a commendation from the acting governor of the Idaho Territory. It seems Raider saved his life after all."

"Now look here," Pinkerton cried. "Raider is just another agent around this office. He has to abide by the same rules of procedure as the others. If he doesn't write a report for each case, why, we'll dock his wages. Or better yet, we'll hold them up until he sends in a report."

Wagner was trying not to smile. "Whatever you say, sir."

"This agency is not in the business of brutalizing anyone," Pinkerton went on. "I realize a certain amount of force may be necessary to apprehend those who are disrespectful of the law . . ."

"I quite agree, sir."

"But no one, not even Raider, will use that force carelessly."

"No, sir. Not even Raider."

Pinkerton steamed for a few moments and then got out of his chair. "It's time to get some sleep, William. After all, today is Sunday. And I don't want to be late for church."

"Yes, sir."

Pinkerton started for the door, but then turned to regard his associate. "I meant what I said, William. About controlling Raider."

Wagner nodded.

"And William . . ."

"Yes, sir?"

"Keep up the good work."

Pinkerton turned and left the room.

Wagner sighed, taking off his spectacles again for a nervous cleaning. He was a bit worried. Keeping up the good work was no problem for him. But controlling Raider was another matter entirely. The big man from Arkansas had his own methods for solving tough cases, even if those methods often conflicted with agency procedures.

Still, Raider always got the job done. Even if he did make everyone nervous about it. Wagner planned to keep up the good work, but he knew that there was no way he would ever be able to control the rough-and-tumble agent with the big Peacemaker on his hip.

FOUR

Raider managed to swing the butt of the Winchester upward, but not before the diving man cut him. The tip of the blade caught him somewhere on the head. Raider was not sure exactly where, till the sudden warm flow of thick blood down his cheek indicated a laceration above his right eye.

Still, the butt of the rifle found its mark, slamming into the guts of the lunging knife man. He grunted as Raider poled him over his shoulder, sending him flying toward the hard ground. When he hit, Raider levered the Winchester, sure that he would have to blast the man and alert the Dog man—if he wasn't alerted already.

He took aim as the man squirmed on the ground.

But he couldn't bring himself to fire.

The knife-wielding assailant seemed to be wrestling with himself. He rolled his head back at the big Pinkerton, his countenance agape with the certain horror of death. Raider squinted to see where the man had his hands. They were closed around the hilt of the knife, which was now lodged in his stomach. Blood poured out between his fingers.

He had fallen on top of the blade.

His mouth opened to scream, but his lungs only emptied for the last time.

Raider wheeled back toward the corral. The horses weren't making any noise. They had taken the death of the last man in stride. Raider wondered how they would feel about the capture of the man who had stolen them.

"Stupid," he muttered to himself. "Horses don't think."

It was time to go get Dog Ruben.

When he crept up to the window of the adobe hut, Raider looked in on a spectacle that was surely the source of the bizarre nickname for Ruben Mijares, horse thief. The swarthy outlaw, who didn't look anything like a dog, had the woman on all fours, pumping her from behind like the dawn would never come again.

Raider saw the images there before him, only something didn't look right. The woman's backside seemed fuzzy. Her skin looked too dimpled. And the dog man didn't look right either in the morning shadows.

Mijares sure as hell seemed to be having a good time, though. He hadn't heard all the ruckus with his men, nor a single whinny from the corral. No damned wonder. He was grunting like a bull dog with his teeth in a roast. And the woman was cursing him under her breath, hating the whole thing.

Why the hell did they look so dim? Maybe it was the morning light. No matter. He still had a job to do.

"Hold it right there, Ruben. Don't move another inch."

The outlaw froze, turning his face away.

Why didn't it look right?

"Help me," the woman moaned.

"I aim to, ma'am. Ruben, you just move away and put your hands up. That way I won't have t' kill you."

Mijares called out something in Spanish.

"Nope," Raider said. "There ain't nobody t' help you. I took care of that, amigo. See, I'm a Pinkerton agent, been hired t' bring you back t' Tucson t' stand trial. Hell, I reckon they still hang horse thieves there. That's about all you got t' look forward to, Ruben."

Mijares reached for something.

Raider had no choice. He had to shoot. He squeezed the trigger and fired straight at the image in front of him.

Glass shattered and Ruben seemed to disappear. Pistol fire followed. Slugs whizzed over Raider's head. He dived for the ground, landing with a thud on his stomach. Too late Raider realized he had fired not at Mijares but at his reflection in a mirror.

Ruben was scrambling inside, screaming in Spanish. He was crying something about this being Mexico, that Raider couldn't take him back. His pistol exploded several more times at the window. The woman kept on screaming too.

Raider heard something slam. He got up and started toward

the corral. Dog Ruben was running naked for the hay shed, his pistol waving in the air. Raider sighted in, squeezed one shot, but missed as Ruben went flying into the corral gate.

What was the son of a bitch going to do now?

Raider levered the '76 and fired again, missing as the slug slammed into the wood of the corral.

Ruben was going to do it. He was going to let the horses go. Raider took aim once more, but it was too late. The gate was swinging open and the stolen remuda began to stampede out of the corral.

Dog Ruben intended to give it one good shot. He grabbed the neck of a chestnut mare and swung up onto her bare back. Raider had a good look at him, even with the horses spilling out all around.

The Winchester barked three times.

Dog Ruben clutched his arm and went down, falling into the hooves of the stampeding remuda.

The horses swung around the house, running back toward the river.

Raider watched them go, wondering if he would be able to catch any of them later. The ranchers wouldn't be too happy if he came back with nothing but a body slung over a pack horse. They wanted their animals as well as the man who stole them.

But that would have to wait.

When the remuda had dispersed, Raider walked over to the limp body that lay on the ground. Dog Ruben's head had been caved in by the hooves of the remuda. Raider's rifle shot had also taken a sizeable chunk out of his arm. The big man had to give it to Mijares, the outlaw had been spirited right up to the end.

He turned away, taking a deep breath, looking back at the horses that were splashing in the river. Most of the animals had stopped to drink, following the big roan stallion. Maybe they just couldn't bring themselves to stray far from the smell of hay and oats.

Raider started to close the gate but then saw that the other side of the corral had been knocked down in the confusion. Some of the horses had pushed in the opposite direction, spilling out from the hole in the fence.

"Lordy."

He remembered he had left the two men tied there. He hurried to help but as soon as he saw the bodies he stopped. Both of them had been trampled. Nothing to do now but bury the corpses. Or take them back to Arizona.

Then he heard the woman's cry.

She was standing over the body of Dog Ruben, kicking the dead carcass with her bare feet. Cursing in Spanish. She was naked as well, a large body with full curves, dark skin.

Raider shook off the sudden urge and went to help her.

Raider wrapped her in a blanket and then started a fire in the hearth of the adobe hut.

She was pretty. Big eyes and thick lips. Black hair.

But Raider didn't have the inclination. She had been through a rough time and he had no intention of making it rougher.

"What's your name?"

She looked down into the fire. "Lucia."

He wished he had some coffee to offer her, but he didn't feel like searching through the filth of the slapdash hacienda. "You from Nogales?"

Lucia grunted hatefully. "I am from a place you have never heard of."

"Well, I can take you back there when we're finished."

She spat into the fire and cursed the name of Ruben Mijares. "I have no home. Ruben burned it down. He killed everyone because I did not want to go with him."

Raider sighed, knowing he had to go round up those horses before he slept. "Killed your whole family, did he?"

"Not that kind of family," she replied. "It was a house. You know the ones. I'm sure you have been to them before."

Raider nodded. "Ruben was a bad one. But he ain't nothin' now. An' don't fret, Lucy. I'm gonna take you someplace where you'll be all right. By the way, how'd you get hooked up with a bandido like Ruben anyway?"

She shrugged. "He used to come see me. He fell in love with me. But after a while, I didn't want to do it with him, even when he paid me."

"Hmm. Well, I ain't never been one t' trust love very much. I guess this just proves out my suspicions."

"Men are wolves and beasts."

He only nodded. Best not to argue with that one. Besides, he knew she was right.

He got up, stretching.

Lucia looked up at him with wide eyes. "Where are you going?"

"Gotta get them horses, put 'em back in that corral."

"But what shall I do?"

He gestured toward the fire. "Cook somethin', I guess. I'm so hungry I could eat the ass-end of a raw gopher."

"But what will I cook?"

He told her to round up a rooster.

"An' I gotta sleep before we get packin'," he said.

She frowned at him.

"No, don't worry," he assured her. "I ain't gonna expect you t' bed down with me. Besides, I ain't got the strength."

She stood up. "Your head. It's bleeding."

Raider touched the dried line of blood on his face. He had forgotten about the knife wound. It must have been a small cut.

Lucia confirmed this by dabbing away the blood with a wet cloth. "Only a tiny slit. But it bled a lot."

Raider drew away from her. She still smelled like a woman, even after all she had been through. And the blanket had fallen half open, revealing the dark canyon of her bosom.

"Cover up," he told her. "An' see if you can find somethin' t' eat in this shack."

"I will."

He started away.

"Gringo?"

He looked back, his black eyes glassy with exhaustion. "My name is Raider. I'm a Pinkerton agent."

"Thank you," she said bashfully. "Thank you for helping me."

"You ever been across the border?" he asked.

"No."

"Want t' go?"

She nodded.

"Okay, just work with me and we'll be out o' here in no time. But we got t' do it right, so we don't lose them horses."

She smiled. "I will do it right."

After one last look at her, he left the hut to round up the horses.

Most of the remuda stood in the river, drinking the fresh water from the St. Miguel. When Raider approached with the lariat, the big roan immediately came out to challenge him. Raider was about ten yards away when the stallion made the first threatening move. It reared, laying back its ears and baring its teeth. This was exactly what Raider wanted.

As the stallion rose up, the big man swung the lasso in the air a couple of times before launching the loop straight at the stallion's head. The rope fell over the roan as it dropped its feet back to earth. Raider tightened the noose and snubbed the end of the rope around a slim tree nearby, hoping it would be strong enough to hold. He expected the animal to fight him all the way, but the stallion only pawed at the ground a couple of times before it settled right down. The big man was puzzled until he remembered that the horses weren't exactly wild. They had been stolen from the best stock in Arizona, so it made sense that they were used to being handled.

"Come on, honcho. Let's see how many o' these mares follow you home."

He looped the rope around the horse's nose, fashioning a crude halter, and led the roan back into the corral, tying the rope to the fence. About thirty horses followed the stallion into the corral, with another twenty or thirty hesitating just outside the fence. Raider considered fixing the broken fence, but then decided on something a little easier.

Going to the hay shed, he broke open bags of oats and spread them in the feeding troughs around the corral. The smell of fresh grain lured them back into the corral. He added a couple of hay bales for the steeds that did not trust his offering of oats.

By midday, he counted eighty head in the corral, which meant that a few horses were still wandering nearby. Maybe they'd join in when he started north with the remuda. It had been a long time since he had driven horses by himself. He wondered if he could handle the whole herd. He'd just have to try. The horses had to be back over the border before he could rightly claim that he had rescued them.

He remembered his own mount, the broken-down grey that

had served him so well on the trek south. Striding back along the river bank, he found the animal standing, dozing, where he had tied him. He led him back to the hay shed and fed him.

Damn, he thought, looking back at the corral. A hundred head to manage by himself. Maybe the woman could help, although it was a safe bet that she didn't know a damned thing about herding horses. Raider wasn't sure he'd be so good at it himself. Maybe he'd just keep that roan on a tether, use him for a Judas goat and get the other animals to follow him north.

He decided not to feel too satisfied with his handiwork. The trip back over the border was going to be another adventure in itself. No telling who he would run into in the wilds of the Mexican plain. Any bandido with three or four men to back him up would want to try for the horses.

Maybe he should just leave them, head back to Nogales, and get word to the ranchers where they could find their horses. That'd go over big with the men who were paying for his services. But hell, even if he did get word to the ranchers, they'd still have to cross the border to claim their property. By that time, some fortunate pistolero would happen along and take the remuda for himself.

No more thinking, he told himself. Just sleep. That was what he needed more than anything. When he had rested, the whole thing would be a lot clearer.

As Raider turned back toward the adobe hut, he saw smoke rising from the crude chimney. Maybe the woman had cooked something for him. A big plate of beans and fatback would look good. His long legs carried him back toward the house.

Dog Ruben was still lying in the yard. His compañeros were also lying in the sun. It would be a while before they started stinking. By that time, Raider would have them in the ground.

When his massive frame filled the doorway of the hut, the woman turned to look at him with her big brown eyes. A half smile parted her thick lips. She had been stirring a stewpot over the hot fire. Beads of perspiration had formed on the ridge of her mouth.

"I found the rooster," she said.

Raider nodded. "I reckon you did." He glanced around the hut. "Looks like you cleaned up around this dump too."

She looked bashfully away. "I combed my hair as well."

Raider tried to keep from smiling. Women were funny that way. You could drag them through hell rescuing them and they'd come up worrying about the way they looked.

"Smells good," he said, glancing at the kettle.

"There were potatoes and onions," Lucia replied. "Some salt too. I hope you like it."

Raider sat down on a wooden chair as she spooned the steaming repast into a wooden bowl. He ate quickly, thanking her between mouthfuls. As soon as he was full, his eyes began to grow heavy. He was half-aware of Lucia as she helped him down to the pallet on the floor.

A deep, dreamless slumber overtook him, and it was only when he awoke hours later in the darkness that he realized the woman was sleeping next to him.

FIVE

He smelled her hair even before he opened his eyes. She was butted up next to him, her ass rubbing against the tumescent shaft that bulged inside his jeans. Lucia moved slightly, brushing his cock with her firm backside. He started to touch her shoulder, but something inside his head stopped him. Maybe she had just crawled in with him to keep warm.

But what the hell was he going to do about the rigid nuisance that felt Lucia's body pressing against it?

Maybe if he got up to take a leak.

Or went outside and did something about himself, like he had to do when he had been on the trail too long.

She smelled like wet cactus flowers.

Damn her anyway for getting into his bed. What was she really? Just some hot-pants Mexican chippy who had probably been bought by every wrangler and *juajero* on both sides of the border. Still, he had to consider what she had been through. And experience told him that if he considered a woman's feelings ten times, she might just consider his wants and needs once or twice.

She sure smelled good though. He brushed his face against her hair, a minor indulgence before he got up to take matters into his own hands—or hand. His fingers touched her shoulder, soft and smooth.

Lucia emitted a slight moan.

"Okay," Raider said. "I'll leave you alone. Maybe now that I slept some, I can figure out what to do next."

"The horses," he said aloud. "I better go make sure they're safe."

He started to get up.

Lucia reached for him, grabbing his hard cock. "No. The horses can wait."

Raider didn't even have to think twice about lying back down. He reclined on the pallet, asking her if she maybe had second thoughts. She replied that she was not thinking at all. She only wanted him inside her.

Her skilled fingers loosened the buttons of his fly.

"I felt you against me," she said. "Now I want you. I . . . *madre*!"

Her brown eyes widened when she removed the length of swollen timber from his jeans. She began to jerk him up and down, rubbing both hands on the massive erection. Raider reached up to touch her backside, feeling the soft curves of her ass.

"Get on top o' me," he urged.

She obeyed without hesitation, straddling his crotch. He watched as she guided his prickhead to the opening of her dark cunt. He felt her warmth and her moistness as she took him inside her.

Lucia took a deep breath. She stopped, sitting there on top of him. Raider closed his eyes. His whole body was on fire.

She started to move, swaying her hips as much as her fixed position would let her. Slowly, up and down, squishing as he went in and out. Raider touched her stomach, running his hands up to her large breasts. Her nipples hardened when he cupped her bosom.

"So big," she moaned. "All of it. You are a good man."

Raider wasn't about to debate the tentative truth of that statement. He had other ideas. Like doing things his way.

"Now I want you to lay down, Lucy."

"A moment more."

She hastened her motion, closing her eyes, rolling her head back. Raider felt her shiver and she sat down again, whimpering, keeping him locked inside her. She bit her lip, grimacing.

"You okay?" he asked softly.

She nodded. "It was just so deep. It's never been deep like that before. I've had big ones, but never did I shake so deep."

Raider urged her off him. "Let's see if we can shake it a little more."

He rolled her onto her back. Lucia spread her round, dark thighs, holding her hand up to him. Raider fell on top of her, prodding her wetness with the tip of his manhood. She gasped when he found the mark, pushing into her with one quick stroke.

Lucia gave a groan that sounded like a wounded animal. But her face was drawn up in an expression of pleasure, not pain. She wrapped her legs around Raider's torso, trying to pull him down to kiss him.

Raider pressed his mouth to hers, meeting her tongue with lapping strokes of his own. They began to move, a man and a woman who knew about the acrobatics of physical love. Raider kept his hips driving until the release rose inside him. When he collapsed into her, plunging his length to the hilt, she cried out with throaty bursts of ecstasy, experiencing her own climax.

He pushed his face into her breasts, licking the erect nipples, tickling her with his mustache.

"So deep, cowboy."

"You just about saved this ol' cowboy's life, honey. I never figured you'd want it after that . . ."

She chortled derisively. "Ruben? That pig. I'm glad he's dead. I felt bad for a while, but now I am all right. I just wish he hadn't burned the house down. Where will I go?"

Raider shrugged. "That could be easy, I mean, dependin' on what you want t' do. You ever been to Tucson?"

She sighed, shaking her head. "I could be a whore there, is that what you mean? A Mexican whore in Arizona."

Raider felt sort of helpless. "Well, puddin', what else d' you have in mind? I mean, unless you want t' get married or somethin'."

She looked up into his black eyes. "Would you marry me?"

"Ah . . ." Raider rolled off her, lying next to her on the pallet. "Honey, you don't want me. I ain't the type t' keep a wife happy."

She sighed again. "I know. I just thought I'd ask."

"But I will take you t' Tucson with me. That is, if you want t' go."

"Sure. Why not?" Her tone was somewhat defeated.

He tried to change the subject. "You know anything about wranglin' horses, Lucy?"

Her hand closed around the moist limpness between his legs. "No, this is the only thing I know about." She took his prickhead into her mouth.

"Lucy . . ."

But what could he say? She worked on him until he was hard again. He tried to get her to lie back, but she shook her head.

"Like a dog," she whispered.

Raider frowned. "After Mijares, you want to . . ."

"I hated Ruben," she replied. "But I love you. And I want it that way. Will you?"

Nothing to do but oblige her.

He positioned himself behind her, guiding his length into her wet crevice. She rocked back, her voluptuous body trembling with each thrust of his hips. Raider kept on for a while but he couldn't concentrate, so he had her stretch out on her back again.

Lucia grunted, her body tensing when he entered from above. He felt her tightening and his own climax came just as quick. He collapsed again, kissing her on the neck and shoulders. He was nuzzled against her voluptuous breasts when he fell asleep.

The next thing he knew, it was morning and Lucia was awake, yelling for him to come to the window.

Raider glanced up at the distressed señorita. "What the hell is wrong with you, honey?"

"Men," she replied. "*Federales*."

"Shit!"

Raider jumped up, buttoning his jeans. He stepped to the crude casement and peered out toward the men in light brown uniforms. They were carrying single-shot rifles on lanyards, draped over their shoulders like a third arm. Raider counted ten of them, including a smart-looking sergeant.

He looked back at his guns and sighed deeply.

"You cannot kill them!" Lucia cried.

Raider nodded. "You're damned right 'bout that."

Ten to one didn't shape up as good odds in the big man's favor.

"Shit!"

Two soldiers were dragging the body of Dog Ruben Mijares across the yard. Another group of men were calling that they had found the bodies of his compañeros. The sergeant regarded everything with a discerning eye before he turned and started toward the hut.

Lucia grabbed Raider's arm. "Cowboy, the federales can be worse than Ruben and his men."

"Don't you think I know that?"

And here he was in Mexico, a long way from home. What if the damned sergeant was a cousin of Dog Ruben Mijares? Raider might spend the rest of his days busting rock in some Mexican prison.

"We can run," Lucia offered as the sergeant drew closer.

Raider grunted. "To where? My grey is in the hay shed. Even if we lit out on foot, they'd see us and catch us in a hurry."

"They're going to catch us anyway."

Raider started for the door. "Maybe I can do some fancy talkin'. Come on, woman. He might not speak English."

As Raider suspected, the sergeant spoke only Spanish. He stopped when Raider and Lucia came out of the hut. But he did not take his rifle off his shoulder. He simply barked some rapid-fire commands that prompted his men to take aim at Raider.

"Tell him I ain't lookin' for trouble," the big man said.

Lucia translated and then gave him the reply. "He wants to know if you are the one who killed Mijares."

Raider nodded, unsure what the flashy-eyed Mexican was going to do. He wished for a moment that he had his Colt, but then realized that they probably would have shot him on sight had he been carrying a gun. He held up his hands so everyone could see he was unarmed.

The sergeant said something else to Lucia.

She raised an eyebrow, but then said to Raider. "He was coming here to buy horses from Ruben."

Raider kept smiling. "What else did he say?"

Lucia grinned. "He thinks I am pretty."

"Tell 'im Mijares stole them horses," Raider offered. "Tell 'im I came t' take 'em back t' Arizona where they belong."

Lucia flirted a bit while she told him.

The sergeant smiled at her, but then frowned at Raider, replying in a doleful voice.

Lucia shook her head. "He does not care who the horses belong to or where they came from. He had a deal with

Ruben. He does not care if you killed him. But he still needs the horses."

Raider saw the sergeant staring at Lucia's breasts under the blanket that draped her body like a poncho. Maybe he'd listen to reason. He seemed like a sympathetic sort.

"Tell 'im it's my job t' bring those horses back," Raider said. "Tell 'im I can't let 'im have 'em."

As she translated, the sergeant only smiled politely, taking off his hat as he replied.

Lucia shook her head. "He says he knows you are in a difficult spot, but he has to take the horses. He also has a deal. His superiors have trusted him to get mounts for a fair price. He says to beg his pardon, but he does not believe you are in a position to tell him he can't take the horses. After all, you are a gringo and this is Mexico. He says he will let you go back without being harmed, but he cannot let you take the horses."

The sergeant started to turn away, offering a polite arm to Lucia.

Raider grabbed him and spun him back, glaring into his surprised countenance. "Tell 'im he has t' deal with me. Now."

She told the sergeant.

He drew away from Raider's grasp.

The others aimed their rifles at him.

"Tell 'im I killed Mijares, so the horses are mine now."

She repeated it as fast as he could say it.

"Tell 'im if he's an honorable gentleman, that he will stand by his bargain an' give me the fair price he was offerin' Mijares."

The sergeant listened curiously and then waved off the rifles. He said something to Lucia in Spanish. She laughed a little and turned to Raider.

"Come with him," she said playfully. "He will count the horses and pay you for them."

Raider exhaled, hoping the bluff had really worked. It would be better to take back something, a few pesos at least. That was a whole lot better than a cock and bull story with nothing to show for his efforts.

The sergeant walked ahead of them, relaying orders to his men.

Lucia pulled back to whisper to Raider. "You really got him on the thing about honor."

"That's 'bout all I had left," the big man replied.

Lucia laughed. "I know what the sergeant is doing. He wants to buy stolen horses so he can claim a higher price when he goes to his superiors for the money."

"There is some mighty fine horseflesh in that corral. Let's just hope he doesn't decide t' shoot me."

"He won't," Lucia assured the big man. "Not with me here. I know his type. Probably straight as an arrow. Religious."

"Not so religious t' keep 'im from cheatin' his own army."

"Ah, that is different," she said matter-of-factly. "He's only making a profit for himself. And the army gets what it pays for."

At the edge of the corral, the soldiers had finished counting the horses. The sergeant did some figuring and then took out a leather pouch from inside his uniform coat. American double eagles, Raider thought as the sergeant dropped three of the twenty-dollar gold coins in his hand. Maybe Dog Ruben had demanded to be paid in American money. Raider fought the urge to ask the soldier where he had gotten so many gringo gold pieces.

He offered sixty dollars to the big man from Arkansas.

"Shit," Raider replied, refusing to take the money. "Tell him that's only a dollar a head."

Lucia told him and then translated the reply. "He says that is the deal he had with Ruben."

"Then ask him why he brought such a large bag of gold."

The sergeant raised an eyebrow when the question was posed to him.

"He says he will shoot you," Lucia offered after the sergeant's hostile reply.

Raider smiled. "Yeah. Well tell 'im that he'll have t' lie awake at night, thinkin' 'bout how he cheated me. His chest will be full of gold, but that won't get 'im into heaven."

Lucia went on for a while, embellishing her translation with things that Raider did not rightly understand. She even went as far as to pull the sergeant aside and whisper something into his ear. Her shucking seemed to bring him around, because he relented almost immediately and tossed the bag of gold coins to Raider.

"Six hundred dollars American," Lucia said. "That was his deal with Mijares. That will be his deal with you."

Raider only nodded. Ten dollars a head wasn't that great a price for sixty horses, but it wasn't bad either. He made Lucia tell the sergeant that the grey in the hay shed was his own personal mount.

The sergeant, through the woman, replied that he did not care about the grey. He only wanted to take his horses and go. Raider was on his own after the money changed hands. The big man agreed that was proper.

He wondered about Lucia, until she made it clear that she was going to ride south with the sergeant. Already she was regaling the handsome soldier with perilous tales of her abduction from a fine family, the subsequent murder of her relatives, and the loss of the family estate and fortune. Raider figured she'd make a good wife for a soldier. She'd be safe and at least he wouldn't have to drag her along on the trip north.

He hefted the pouch of double eagles. The ranchers would just have to be happy with six hundred bucks. Unless he could come up with something else to sweeten the pot. But that would have to wait until the federales were no longer in sight.

The big man from Arkansas wondered if the sergeant might have a couple of his men double back to take the money from him. After they rode off to the south, he found some cover and watched the trail for a while. When nobody came, he saddled the grey and started along the river. He hoped to find some of the animals that had strayed out of the remuda when Dog Ruben started the stampede. A few horses would be the pot sweetener along with the bag of double eagles.

Raider might have considered keeping the gold for himself, but he was not the kind to trust wealth that was unearned or unwon in a game of chance. Stolen money usually led to more trouble, at least as far as Raider could see. He had run down more than one boy who had figured to get rich by robbing somebody—Dog Ruben Mijares had been a good example. His stealing had led him to a bad end.

With some luck, the big man had rounded up twenty stray

horses by midday. That amounted to less than a fourth of the original number stolen, but the ranchers would just have to live with it. A score of animals and the bag of gold. He started north, hoping like hell that nobody would try to take either one of them away from him.

A week later, dusty and tired from the ride, Raider sat down in front of the Tucson Rancher Association, five glum-looking men who glared at the big Pinkerton like they didn't trust him.

One of them demanded to know where their horses were.

Raider told them slowly, trying to make it sound convincing. But he wouldn't have believed the story himself, had he not lived it. They didn't really seem to believe him either.

"Wait a minute," bellowed a fat man in a new suit. "That sounds like hogwash to me."

Raider hated fat men in suits.

"Yeah," said another. "How do we know he's tellin' the truth?"

Fat men in suits were always making demands.

"We hired you to bring back our horses."

Raider exhaled, feeling distant and unmoved. "Gents, you hired me t' stop the man who was rustlin' your ranches. His name was Ruben Mijares, called Dog by some."

He was tempted to tell them why they called him *Dog*.

"Where's this Mijares now?" one of them demanded.

"The federales buried 'im," the big man replied. "I shot him off a horse and he was killed in the stampede he started."

"Horse manure!"

"Yeah," Raider rejoined, "there was plenty o' that around. But it happened just like I told you."

One of the fat, suited men took a little calmer approach. "Now look here, Raider. You say the federales just up and seized those stolen animals?"

He shook his head, suddenly tired of the whole thing. "Not exac'ly, sir. I brought back twenty horses that got away when Mijares stampeded 'em in the first place. They're down at the livery at the end o' town. Just ask the marshal. I checked with 'im after I rode in. Here . . ." He took something from his vest pocket. "The livery man signed for 'em. Here's the proof. You all go down an' claim your brands."

"Pshaw!" bellowed the original fat man. "Twenty horses out of a hundred. You expect that to satisfy us?"

Raider glared at the man. "I don't expect you to do nothin', Chief. I put my ass on the line down there with those federales. They didn't want t' give me nothin', but I held out for this!"

He threw the bag of gold on the table. The pouch opened and the coins spilled out in front of the ranchers' eyes. That got their attention. Gold always enraptured greedy men—hell, even men who weren't so greedy.

The original fat man looked up again. "How do we know he's not lying? There were almost a hundred horses in that lot. What if the Mexicans gave him fifty dollars a head and he's holding out?"

"Would he have come back here to face us if he had five thousand dollars?" offered the calm gentleman.

Three of the others suggested that Raider had done a good enough job. He had assured them that Mijares was dead and he had done his best to retrieve their property. Perhaps they should split the money and be happy. Six hundred wasn't full market value for the animals, but it was close enough.

Raider stood up. "You gents are welcome t' write t' my agency an' complain. I have t' report to 'em myself, an' b'lieve me, I ain't that happy 'bout it. I ain't happy 'bout losin' most o' your horses or 'bout takin' that gold or 'bout goin' into Mexico without permission. But I think there's some ol' sayin' 'bout birds in hand bein' worth more 'n birds in the bush. If I were y'all, I'd heed that sayin' and be thankful you got a little bit o' the bird back in hand."

With that, he took his leave. As he went, he could hear them still arguing behind him. That was what money did to a man. It turned him into a weak-livered, chair-sitting, fat-bellied child. He wanted to laugh at the whole thing, but their greed disgusted him too much.

He stomped downstairs, into the street, heading for the hotel.

He saw a dark-haired woman and he immediately thought of Lucia. How the hell was she doing with the sergeant? She had saved his ass. Of course, he had saved her ass first. He only wished she was there to share it with him.

Maybe there were some Mexican whores in Tucson, even

if the town was getting a little bit uppity for him. Citizens' Committees and Rancher Associations always managed to put a stranglehold on the fun doings that a gunman required. But gambling and whoring were quickly becoming things of the past in Tucson. Pretty soon a man would have to ride all the way to Nogales to have a good time.

"Raider!"

The call had come from inside a saloon.

The big man from Arkansas stopped at the swinging doors and peered in. He saw the bartender waving at him. He couldn't place the face at first.

"Raider, it's me! Big Jim."

That rang a bell, so Raider pushed into the saloon.

It took some small reminding before Raider realized who he was talking to. Big Jim Claremont had been a Pinkerton himself, until he decided to leave the service, get married, and buy a saloon. He kept pouring shots of red-eye, glad to quiz Raider on the last five years.

"So," Big Jim said finally, "where the hell is Doc Weatherbee? He's usually doggin' your steps, raggin' on you about too much drinkin'."

Raider grimaced. "Doc got the bug just like you. Met a girl he couldn't handle an' up an' married 'er. Livin' in Chicago now."

Big Jim guffawed. "Lordy be. I reckon it happens to all of us sooner or later. When you gonna take the plunge, Raider?"

"Soon as somebody invents a woman that don't nag, don't make demands, don't try to change a man, don't try to . . ."

"Whoa," Big Jim said, smiling, "them first three would be hard enough. I reckon you're sayin' you ain't never gonna settle down."

Raider sighed. "No, I reckon not."

"Pity."

Raider squinted at his old friend. "Why you say that?"

"Oh, I don't know. I reckon a jailbird like me can't stand to see a free man. And that's what you are, Raider. Free. Plain and simple."

The big man from Arkansas took another shot of whiskey, considering what Big Jim had said. It made him feel sort of happy and sort of sad at the same time. Sure, he was free. But free for what? To chase down bad men, to kill the ones who were killing, to steal the lives of those who stole.

"Hey," Big Jim said, "you look down in the mouth, partner."

Raider offered a big, forced coyote grin. "Naw, not me, Jim. I'm as happy as a pig in shit."

He slammed the shot glass on the table. "Hit me again."

Big Jim poured the glass full. "Who you workin' with these days?"

"By myself."

Big Jim stared at him in disbelief. "You mean the old man lets you work without a partner?"

Raider nodded. "Yep. But I ain't gonna worry 'bout it right now, Jim. 'Cause I'm free. You said it yourself. Free as hell."

"You're a little drunk, too."

"That I am. An' I plan t' get drunker. Then I plan t' go find me a hot bath, an even hotter steak, an' a woman that makes 'em both look like ice on a Rocky Mountain peak. An' after that—well hell, you never know what a free man from Arkansas will do."

Big Jim watched as his old colleague proved true to his word. Raider drank until he almost could not stand. Then he started out of the saloon, weaving a little, but still proud and tall. It was kind of sad on one hand, Big Jim thought. But then again, it was good to see such spirit in a man. He just hoped Raider didn't get into anything that would land him in trouble.

Of course, trouble had a way of finding the tall, rough-hewn Pinkerton all by its lonesome.

SIX

William Wagner found himself in a bit of a dilemma. He had been wrestling with it for three weeks, since his last communiqué from Raider. So far he had kept the documents—for there were subsequent messages—from Allan Pinkerton, but he knew that sooner or later the top man was going to ask for an evaluation of Raider's current situation. Wagner was not sure he wanted to be the one to tell him what had transpired.

Oddly, Wagner had figured Raider was on the road to shaping up when he received his report on the Tucson horse-thief caper. It had obviously been penned by someone else (the handwriting was impeccable); but the report went into great detail, including a couple of things that had bothered Wagner immediately.

Of prime concern was Raider's incursion into Mexico. He had gone over the border without permission from the agency, not to mention both sides of the government. He had dealt with someone else's property instead of taking the thing through proper channels. The big man from Arkansas had acted without regard for procedure, something that was not new to him.

Also evident in the report was Raider's arrogance toward and rude treatment of the ranchers. Wagner was not sure that Pinkerton would approve of the agency being represented in such a manner. True, Raider was probably tired and hungry, bushed from his mission. But that did not make it all right for him to show disrespect to the men who were paying for his services.

Wagner wondered why Raider had suddenly chosen to give the details of his adventure. Usually the reports were terse and crude. But his latest account led Wagner to believe that his roughest agent had finally started to smooth out some of his edges.

That thought, however, was soon dispelled.

Wagner suspected the change had something to do with Raider's back pay. Since he had not drawn his wages for three months, Raider had nearly five hundred dollars coming to him in retroactive salary. The sly rascal had known it, too, and he wanted to see that he got it. Hence, the polished report, followed by a modest request for "any pesos I got coming." Wagner should have been tipped off by the fact that Raider did not request his next assignment.

Playing right into the hands of the Arkansas hillbilly, Wagner had wired permission for Raider to draw all his back pay at the Western Union office. He had also sent along the next assignment for the big man, thinking that Raider would simply do as he was told. But it hadn't worked out that way at all.

Not an hour after he had sent the wire, Wagner received a reply from Tucson. The collect telegram read: "Decided to take me some time off. If you ain't obliged to this, then too bad. I ain't had no time off for almost a year. I will send word when I'm ready to work again. Raider."

Wagner had been nonplussed for a while, but when he got over the arrogance of the message, he realized Raider was right. The big man had not been on a holiday for a long time. And a holiday consisted of three things for Raider: gambling, whiskey, and women, in no particular order. No, the message in itself had not been disconcerting, as Wagner could cover for Raider until he got word from him again.

The problem was the letter.

It had come about two days after Raider drew his back pay. One of the Tucson ranchers had written it. The letter basically accused Raider of stealing their horses and selling them, then giving them only part of the money. The rancher believed that the few horses Raider had brought back were intended to make him look good and avert suspicion from himself. The same held for the bag of gold coins. The rancher contended that Raider had only brought back half of what he had really been given by the federales.

Wagner had been considering the rancher's complaint for nearly a week. In Raider's own account of the incident, he had admitted to dealing with the Mexican soldiers. And Wagner could not imagine the big man stealing something like gold, or even horses. Had Raider seen a mount in the stolen herd that he wanted, he would have offered the rancher a fair price for it. Probably would not take it as a gift if the rancher presented it to him.

Sour grapes, Wagner thought. The rancher had not recovered everything that he thought he had coming to him. Now he wanted to pin the blame on someone, so he had chosen Raider.

Damn that big galoot. Just when Wagner needed him around, he disappeared. Even if several agents were dispatched to look for him, they might not locate the tall man for months. They'd have to check every whorehouse and saloon west of the Mississippi.

"William?"

Wagner looked up to see Allan Pinkerton standing in the doorway of his office. "Yes, sir?"

"I believe we have some reports to go over."

Wagner nodded, picking up all the papers on his desk, including the ones that concerned Raider.

When they had gone through most of the reports, Wagner still nursed a spark of hope that he might be able to avoid discussing Raider. He somehow felt that Raider would turn up to vindicate himself of the rancher's charges. Or, barring the big man's arrival, Wagner could check into a few things himself, try to corroborate Raider's testimony and disprove the rancher's accusations.

But Pinkerton was too sharp to let anything get by him.

He glanced sideways at Wagner and said, "Haven't heard a word about that thorn in my side."

Wagner tried to look puzzled. "I beg your pardon, sir?"

"Let's have it William. You got a file there on Raider?"

There was no way to show further reluctance without being disrespectful, so he told him everything, beginning with the report and ending with the rancher's complaint.

Pinkerton just rubbed his thick beard, listening, pondering. "Where is he now?"

Wagner shrugged. "I don't know, sir. He said he'd get in touch with me."

Pinkerton roared out of his chair. "Get in touch with you!

Who the devil does he think he is? He doesn't run this agency."

"I know, sir, but he did have a vacation coming to him . . ."

Pinkerton waved him off. "That don't wash on the wash-board, William. He's no right to be insubordinate. I know he's done a good job for us, but we have to draw the line."

Wagner knew the worst was coming, but he still felt some strange compulsion to defend Raider. "I thought I'd pursue my own investigation into the matter of the rancher's complaint."

Pinkerton grunted. "What? Oh, very well. But that won't change my mind, William."

"Sir?"

"As of now, Raider is on probation, suspended without pay, pending a hearing with me. As soon as you have word from him, tell him to get his arse to Chicago in a hurry."

"Yes, sir." Wagner paused before he asked the next question. "Mr. Pinkerton, what if we can't vindicate Raider from these charges by the rancher?"

"Then I'm afraid," Pinkerton replied angrily, "that he will have to be suspended permanently."

Wagner gaped at his associate. "You mean *fire* him?"

"Yes," Pinkerton said. "That is precisely what I mean."

SEVEN

If Raider had known his job was in jeopardy, he probably would not have cared. He was free. Flying south on the strong back of the foul-looking grey. He was proud to have such an animal under him. The wind rushed past him. There was no threat, no place to be, nothing to worry about.

The three weeks in Nogales had helped: three weeks of good women, bad gambling, and the worst whiskey known to man. Mostly he had slept in the best bed that money could buy in Nogales. Even with the gambling at faro—the game he hated most and always lost at—he still had slightly more than two hundred dollars in his pocket. Enough for a free man to have some more fun before he sent a message to Chicago saying he wanted to work. He would go back to work.

Wouldn't he?

He had to admit that he liked the free life. No cares, no worries, no cases, no boss to answer to, nobody with guns trying to shoot his ass off. He was feeling something that few men ever felt, that incredible surge of energy that comes with the limitless possibilities of the world. There was a whole country to see again, without chasing somebody over it. Did he really want to work? He kept asking himself that as he drove north.

One last errand to take care of before he rode . . . where? Maybe back to Arkansas, see if he could round up any of his kin. He could stop in El Paso, Austin—anywhere there was whiskey or women. Pick up day work if he needed a few extra bucks.

"Whoo-wee!"

He said it to the wind, galloping north toward a shimmering horizon. Blue summer haze had overtaken the plain. It was warm, but not too hot, as southern Arizona was known to be. The kind of day when a man could fill his lungs without perceiving the unholy stenches of civilization.

"Whoo-wee!"

He hadn't felt so good since he was a pup. There were even a couple of women he was planning to look up. Some might offer him a full-time setup. He'd have to work, but so what? Maybe Big Jim had been right. It happened to everyone sooner or later.

His luck was running good as well. It wasn't long before he saw the bump of the adobe house on the plain. Rodrigo wouldn't be expecting him, but Raider was sure he wouldn't fire once he recognized him. That ran true to his fortune of late. The Mexican was sitting on a stool in front of his house, peeling an onion.

"Señor! You have return. Where are my horses?"

Raider climbed down off thee grey. "We'll get t' that. First I owe you eight dollars for that nag. Here." He gave him eight silver dollars.

Rodrigo clinked the money in his hands. "Señor, let me buy back thee grey. I geeve you eleven dollars for heem."

Raider glanced sideways at the horse trader. "What would I ride?"

Rodrigo gestured toward the corral. "I have a mule. I weell throw eet een weeth thee deal."

"No way, Rigo. That grey don't leave me till it drops."

Rodrigo sighed, going back to his onion. "Well, I guess I am no longer a horse trader. My days they are over. No wan wants to buy a mule."

"I won't buy 'im," Raider said with a mischievous grin, "but I might eat 'im if you was t' cook 'im up."

The Mexican glared at the big man. "Eet ees not funny. I lost everything to the Dog."

"I bought the grey at least."

"Not even enough to pay for my coffin," Rodrigo lamented.

Raider thought about it for a while. "How many head you lose to the Dog man?"

Rodrigo shrugged. "Ten horses."

"All right. What if I said I could help you get twenty head?"

Rodrigo sat up and took notice. "Twenty horses!"

The big man pointed south. "Dog Ruben took more'n a hundred head down t' the St. Miguel. I brought twenty back with me. Had to take 'em all back t' Tucson. Had brands on 'em. The federales took sixty head with 'em. That leaves another twenty or more head not 'counted for."

"Ay Chihuahua!" Rodrigo cried. "I believe you. But do you steell theenk we can find those horses after all thees time?"

Raider had a gleam in his eye, a pounding in his heart. "I'm willin' t' go take a look."

"I weell ride thee mule," Rodrigo declared. "And believe me, señor. If we can find twenty horses, I will make at least two hundred dollar!"

"Deal," Raider said, feeling right and strong.

"You will see, señor. If you can find thee horses."

"Funny country down there," Raider said. "You never can tell what you're gonna come across."

The old devil was coming out in him. Crossing the border again. But it didn't matter. He felt like a kid going on a Halloween hayride.

Raider waited in the ravine with the Colt drawn. The slow clop of hooves echoed along the hollow concaves of the depression. Up till now, the horse caper had gone perfectly. They managed to find thirty head, no doubt all strays from other runs by Dog Ruben. To top it off, they had also come up with forty-odd head of cattle.

Rodrigo had said he would sell it all, but that Raider could not go with him to do it. So Raider had waited in the ravine, first for a half day and then well into the next morning and afternoon. He couldn't guess as to what had happened to Rodrigo. Bad Indians and loose bandits roamed the borderland without shame or fear of a living soul.

Raider had begun to feel like someone who bought a pig in a poke—until he heard the clop of hooves. Then he was ready with the Colt, the old tension coming back from years of caution in dealing with outlaws. What if bad Indians had killed Rodrigo and were now coming to get him?

"Señor Raider!"

The mule ambled down the center of the ravine. Rodrigo

was waving. A pouch was slung over his shoulder, hanging heavily on his side.

"Señor, we are reech!"

Raider ran down to greet him. "Not so loud, Rigo. I ain't killed nobody in a while an' I don't want t' start with a bunch o' bandits."

Rodrigo took off the pouch and tossed it to the big man. "Five hundred dollar. Go on; take your half."

Raider reached into the pouch, taking out the equivalent portion in gold and scrip. "Damn, Rigo. What the hell did you do?"

"I sold them to the federales," Rodrigo replied.

The hairs stood up on the back of Raider's neck. "Well, that means I'm gettin' the hell out o' here."

"You know the sergeant?"

Raider grimaced. "I know 'im all right. Tell me, did he have a pretty woman with him?"

"Sí, señor. Ah! I see. Thees has to do weeth thee woman!"

Raider stuffed his pockets with his share of the horse money. "I'm long gone from here, Rigo. I got me another grubstake." He tossed the pouch back to the Mexican and then started for the grey.

"Señor, we make great partners. Why don't you . . ."

Raider climbed into the saddle and tipped his hat. "Adios, amigo. You got what was took from you. Far as I'm concerned, this case is closed."

"But where weell you go?"

He turned the horse northeast and called over his shoulder. "El Paso."

The holiday was by no means over for the man who drove the nag as hard as it would run.

EIGHT

Raider didn't think much until he saw Mount Franklin in the distance. El Paso. The Pass. It almost looked beautiful, shimmering with a bluish haze in the heat of summer.

As he came in off the high plains, Raider caught himself starting up a strategy for riding into town. An old habit that had risen out of years of coming into a town to look for somebody. But he wasn't looking for anybody now. He was a horse dealer, if anybody asked.

When he was close enough to make out the flat roofs and plaster walls of El Paso, he reined back on the grey. The town's one street had expanded into a maze of alleys and byways, winding corridors of houses and people. Hadn't he heard something about the railroad coming down this way? It hadn't happened yet, but it was close.

Civilization. Hell; a man couldn't ride five hundred miles anymore without hitting some kind of outpost. And outposts had a way of turning into towns. Pretty soon the whole damned territory would be one big Citizens' Committee. A free man wouldn't have a chance.

So he turned the grey south again, heading for the border. He was getting to like Mexico for some damned reason. Maybe it was a little wilder, a little less predictable. Juarez had plenty of whores too. A man didn't have to knock on a hundred doors before he found a lady willing to take him on for a handful of pesos.

The cantina fell into a hush when Raider filled the shadowed doorway. He was surprised to find it full so early in the afternoon. All the men in the place had their hands moving, anticipating trouble from an hombre the size of the big man from Arkansas. Raider held his hands out in front of him, to show he didn't mean any harm.

Somebody said something in Spanish and the men went back to talking quietly over their wooden mugs of tequila.

Raider walked across the musty cantina, toward a crude bar.

The bartender nodded at him, pouring warm tequila.

Raider drank it down in one gulp and motioned for another.

The bartender gave him another blast, squinting at the grizzled, black-eyed cowboy.

"Good brew," Raider said, downing half the mug.

He put a silver dollar on the counter. "You speak English?"

"Sí, señor."

Raider put another dollar on the bar. "I need a whorehouse. A clean place with a bathtub an' no bedbugs. You *comprende*?"

The man nodded. "Wait. I weell come right back."

Raider drank the tequila while the man was gone. He cast a glance over the barroom, wondering how many of the drinkers were wanted for something on the other side of the border. If he decided to become a bounty hunter, there were plenty of prices on the heads of fugitive outlaws. But somehow that kind of work had never appealed to him.

"Señor?"

The bartender was waving to him. "Come along, señor. You weell need your horse."

Raider followed the small man, riding through Juarez in the heat of the afternoon. His caution would not leave him. Would he always think like a Pinkerton agent? He expected the barkeeper to run him straight into a trap. Get him robbed, maybe murdered.

But the man only led him to a big, white house outside the town limits. A hacienda, complete with a brick wall to discourage intruders. As they passed through the gate, Raider looked up to see the girls lounging on the veranda.

"Yes, sir," he said to the barkeeper. "I'm beginnin' to like Mexico jus' fine!"

"Oww!"

The Mexican girl had poured hot water over Raider's head.

"You have to be clean," she said.

Raider could agree with that, especially when she started to rub him down with a soapy cloth. They were treating him fine at Madam Rosa's. Took care of his horse and his clothes and now his bath. Of course, they had objected when Raider took his guns into the bathhouse with him, but that was one habit he never intended to break. He wanted his firearms close by, in case anything serious came up in a hurry.

"How about rubbin' this?" he said, grinning, trying to pull the girl's hand down to his crotch.

She frowned, which made her unappealing at best. "I am not a whore!" she insisted. "I have to geeve you a bath. Notheeng else."

Raider pointed toward his saddle bag. "Maybe a dollar would ease your mind, honey."

She took the dollar, but still insisted that Raider wasn't going to get anything beyond the bath.

"But ain't you gonna wash my Johnson?" he teased.

"Stand up," she commanded.

Raider obeyed her, rising out of the soapy tub.

The girl took no special notice of his erection. She scrubbed his thighs and his backside. Just as he was giving up hope, she dipped the cloth and pushed it up against his scrotum.

"Don't get excited," she said. "I'm just washing you an' checking you for sores."

It didn't matter to the big man. Her touch excited him. His member expanded under her hand.

He heard laughter and caught three other girls staring at him.

When he called to them, they ran away.

"Get the big boss in here," Raider said. "Pronto."

The girl called Madame Rosa, who came into the bathhouse in a black dressing gown. Her eyes bulged when she saw Raider's prick. She smiled and said something in Spanish.

The girl translated, not smiling at all. "She wants to know eef your father was a horse."

"More like a ass," Raider replied. "Tell her I need t' make arrangements for the week. Food, whiskey, a bed, an' as many whores as I want."

The girl relayed his request with a tone of disapproval.

Madam Rosa only smiled and came back with a counter offer.

"She say twenty dollar a day for you, cowboy. Everytheeng you want."

Raider nodded to her. "Sounds good t' me."

"One condeetion," the girl said.

Raider eyed the frowning lass. "What?"

"Madam Rosa say she want to take a bath with you."

Raider gave his hostess the once-over. She dropped her robe, revealing a full, if somewhat sagging, body. More paint on her face than a peddler's wagon. Raider might have begged off if the throbbing member between his legs had been any less insistent.

He sat back down in the tub. "Hell, if that's what she wants."

Madam Rosa came over the edge of the tub, grabbing his prick, sitting down with a splash in the warm water.

After he had eaten a thick steak with potatoes and onions, Raider settled down into the room provided by Madam Rosa. It was a large, master bedchamber, with thick velvet curtains and a porcelain pisspot. A fresh pitcher and bowl were filled with cool water, and there were clean sheets on the feather bed. A lot to be said for the free life, Raider thought as he climbed into the sack.

He was drifting off to sleep when someone knocked at the door.

Raider slipped his Colt out of the holster that hung on the bedpost. "Come on in."

The young bath girl came through the threshold. She wore a flannel nightgown and had her hair brushed out. Her full, lower lip pouted slightly.

"What the devil do you want?" Raider asked.

She would not look directly at him. "I want you to get on top of me. I want to feel what eet ees like."

Raider scowled at her. "That bath got you all worked up, huh?"

She nodded.

"How old are you girl?"

"Old enough!"

He waved her back toward the door. "Get on outta here."

She refused to go.

Raider hollered for Madam Rosa. When the smiling hostess appeared, Raider gestured to the bath girl. "One o' your virgins is lookin' t' get broke."

Madam Rosa shooed the girl out of the room.

"Get me a fat girl," Raider said. "One that likes to laugh an' drink tequila. One with a sense o' humor."

For a second he wondered if Madam Rosa had understood him. She giggled and went out of the room. Raider was just falling asleep again when the girl arrived at the door. She was full-figured, with large breasts and big brown nipples. She laughed a little as Raider threw back the covers.

Pretty soon, they were both laughing together.

The rest of the week would be like a dream. Until the shooting started.

But the shooting wouldn't come for a while.

Raider settled into the brothel life as if it were the most natural thing in the world. Madam Rosa even let him keep his room during business hours. And there was no shortage of girls. When they all heard about the unnatural length of Raider's pecker, they were practically lined up at the door to have a firsthand look.

Raider's personal preference was the large-breasted girl who had stayed with him the first night. She liked to play little games, like chase and catch. At the end of the game, she would always lie back on the bed, spreading her round thighs for him to enter.

And he would impale her shamelessly, bouncing her off the bed, managing to make her climax over and over, even if he couldn't. He could not remember the last time he stayed hard so much. It was almost beginning to hurt. But the girls were right on the job. They did something with a finger up his bum, massaging the exact spot to make the pain go away and to make him hard again.

After the fifth day of this, he found himself ready for something besides women and tequila. When he suggested that the girls go gambling with him, they promptly formed a game of strip poker, with Raider as the prize. He had to take on four of them at once, which taxed even his reserves.

They fed him after that and then took turns sucking him. A

few of the girls needed instruction in such matters, so Madam Rosa demonstrated on the big man's tumescent shaft. It wasn't exactly boring, Raider thought, but the whole thing was wearing a little thin. He had always suspected that too much of one thing would grow old.

"Raider!"

One of the girls leaned around the door jamb, peering into his room.

The big man was leaning back on the bed, contemplating his exit from Madam Rosa's. "What is it, honey?"

"Dinner."

"Aw, let me rest. I need t' get some shut-eye. We'll play t'night."

She disappeared and Raider closed his eyes.

A few hours later, he was vaguely aware that someone was playing with his cock. He let her play, thinking it was one of the girls. She straddled him, rubbing her lips on his rapidly expanding prickhead.

"Go on," he told her. "Get it over with."

The tightness slipped over his cock, falling about halfway down.

Raider opened his eyes to see the bath girl impaled on his cock. Her pouting face was flushed with ecstasy. She trembled on top of him, her lithe body shaking like an earthquake had hit her.

"Damn you!"

Raider could hear the other girls laughing outside the door.

"Ees too late," the bath girl said. "There's notheeng you can do."

Raider grabbed her little backside. "Oh yes there is."

He flipped her around so she was on her back.

"I'm gonna give you the lesson you was lookin' for."

Her eyes rolled back in her head as he guided his prick into her. She arched her back, lifting her legs. Raider knew the other girls were watching, so he wanted to give them something to be jealous about.

"Take it easy," he urged her. "I ain't gonna give it all t' you at once."

They started slow, working up toward the bed-shaking release at the end.

Raider felt the swelling end of his cock.

"Not een me," the girl said.

He quickly pulled out, spurting the sticky liquid onto her flat stomach.

She reached down with her fingers, dipping them in the semen.

"*Caramba*," she moaned. "Eet was better than I imagined."

Raider just rolled over onto the bedspread.

"Can I touch eet again?" she asked.

Raider nodded. He had never been much for virgins. Somehow it didn't seem right to plug a girl who had never had it before. It sort of made you responsible for her.

"I have washed many of these," the girl said, "but yours ees special. I was waiting for thee right man."

"Honey, I ain't right for nobody, 'specially you."

She laughed, twirling his prick in her fingers. "I don't mean like that. I mean to break me een. I am a whore now."

Raider sighed. "Well, I s'pose I'm happy t' have took part in your education, honey. I ain't never done much o' that sort o' thing, not with a tender girl such as yourself. But then again, I been doin' a lot o' things I ain't never done afore. I reckon 'cause I ain't been workin'."

Working. He tried to remember what it had been like. He wanted the memories to be good, but they weren't. He remembered killing and fighting and shooting and stabbing. He remembered the worst kind of men he had brought to justice. Somehow it made him want to keep moving. It wasn't far to Arkansas, unless you counted the trek across Texas to be a long trip.

"Did he do it, Juanita?"

The other girls had stuck their heads inside Raider's room.

The bath girl nodded. "Eet hurt for a second, but now eet's fine."

Raider winked at her sisters. "Maybe y'all would like t' get in here an' show this little lady some o' your tricks."

He was hard again.

Laughing, the other girls got onto the bed, piling up until the bedboards collapsed. Once they were in a pile, Raider just grabbed whatever came close to his hands. He had his cock in somebody's cunt and he couldn't even tell who it was.

"Whoa, girls, let's get this right."

They all climbed off the collapsed bed.

Raider got up and set it right, putting the bedboards back in place.

Then he took them on one at a time, until they had all gotten enough.

"Now maybe you'll let me sleep."

One of the girls slapped him on the ass and replied, "Hah. Now we have to go to work. It's Saturday night and every juajero in the territory will want to get his nugget wet."

Raider slid under the blanket, pulling the pillow under his head. "Well, that's just breakin' my heart, honey. I reckon I'll have t' sleep through the whole thing."

And he did sleep, until he heard the shouting. Two gunshots followed the loud voices. Running in the house. Raider was reaching for his Colt as the door flew open. He drew back when he saw the pistol pointed at him.

Madam Rosa was standing there with someone behind her.

A woman pushed the madam to the side. "Raider. You son of a bitch."

The big man did not recognize her at first, but he did recognize the Remington .44. "No need to flash that iron, honey. I won't hurt you."

The woman thumbed back the hammer of the .44. "I oughta plug you, Raider."

She wasn't half bad, pretty and full-figured. Nice blue eyes, even if they were narrowed. Full mouth, straight nose.

Raider wondered if she was going to shoot him. "You want t' talk 'bout this afore you kill me?" he asked.

"You better listen if I decide to talk!" she cried.

Raider nodded. He figured it was best to respect a woman with a gun in her hand. At least while she had it pointed at him.

Wagner wasn't happy about the news that had come in from Tucson.

Some cowboy had been spotted in Nogales, carrying a roll of money and calling himself a horse trader. This word had come in from one of his field agents who had been sent to find out what he could about the horse rancher's accusations against Raider.

A description of the cowboy: "Tall, mustache, curly black hair, black eyes, a rugged face."

"Damn him," Wagner said.

Maybe Raider had really stolen horses and gold from the ranchers.

Of course, the roll of money could have been his back pay.

And he might have been calling himself a horse trader so he wouldn't be recognized as a Pinkerton agent.

But there was also word that someone had made a sale of horses and cows to the same federales who had dealt with Raider before.

Everything pointed to the big man's guilt. But Wagner couldn't bring himself to believe Raider would steal anything from anyone. In spite of his shortcomings, Raider still had an honest, God-fearing streak in him that only allowed him to act on behalf of the law. He wasn't a thief.

"William?"

Wagner looked up to see Pinkerton staring down at him.

"Are you all right, William?"

Wagner nodded, lifting a handkerchief to his mouth. "Yes, sir." He coughed. "Just a bit of the croup."

"What's that you're looking at?"

"Man hour reports, sir. Would you like to have a look?"

Wagner held his breath, hoping Pinkerton was in a hurry.

"I haven't time now," Pinkerton replied, turning for his office. "I'll see them tomorrow."

Wagner exhaled, breathing easier. Why the hell was he covering for Raider? And what if Raider turned out to be guilty? Would criminal charges be brought against him?

Raider couldn't be guilty. He wasn't the type. Unless he was getting old. Or crazy.

Wagner felt trapped behind his desk. He would simply have to be satisfied with the work of operatives. Maybe he would put Stokes on it.

"Raider, what have you done?" Wagner groaned.

He would send Stokes to find the federale sergeant. Maybe that would help to clear the big man. Maybe Wagner could find out the truth before all hell broke loose in the agency.

The woman held the Remington steady on him. "Raider, you son of a bitch. You don't even remember me."

The bore of the pistol was helping his memory right along. As the name formed on his lips, he hoped it was the right one. "Tillie?"

Her pretty face slacked and she began to blubber.

"You used to run a house over in El Paso," Raider offered. "I think maybe you and me even . . ."

"I ain't no more!" she cried. "I'm a seamstress. I sew things now. This woman took me in and taught me how, after they burned down the cathouse."

Raider lifted his hands. "Okay, okay. You sew things. That's a right noble undertakin'."

"I make dresses!"

"I bet you do a good job too," he replied.

The tears streaked her round cheeks. As she cried more, the gun became heavier. When she lowered it, Raider climbed out of bed and took it gently from her hand. He put his arm around her shoulder and turned to Madam Rosa.

"Bring whiskey," he said. "Not tequila, but that good stuff you an' me had the other night."

When Tillie had a few drinks in her, she stopped crying.

Raider tried to remember her, but there was little to recall besides her name. Had she always been nice to him? What about the gun?

"How'd you know I was in Juarez?" Raider asked. "An' why'd you come lookin' for me?"

Tillie raised her eyes, suddenly more hopeful. "I'm sorry about the gun, Raider. But I knew they wouldn't let me in without it. I'm a gringo on this side of the border."

He shrugged, resigning to her pleading tone. "Okay, you're forgiven. But how'd you even find me now?"

She looked away, folding her hands together over her bosom. "Raider, I got big trouble. A man."

Raider laughed. "I oughta knowed there'd be a man in this."

"I can't help it!" she cried. "I got a right to fall in love just like everyone else. I mean, seamstressing is okay, but a woman needs excitement."

He had to agree with that. "You always was one for excitement, Tillie."

Or was she? He could remember very little about his past

whoring exploits. The week at Madam Rosa's had blurred everything in his head. But he knew he would remember on the trail, when he was cold and lonely in his bedroll.

"So I still go out at night," Tillie continued. "There's a place where I get together with some of my old girls. They work over on the Mexican side of town. Humping wetbacks and Injuns for a dollar a throw. I can't hold it against them, but . . ."

"Get to the trouble, Tillie."

She sighed, taking a deep breath. "Oh, how come everything starts out so good and then ends up so bad?"

"Bad luck," he said. "So let's hear how it happened. The man, I mean."

She smiled. "He's sweet, Raider, he really is. He was just there one night, with one of the other girls. But we looked at each other and we knew it was meant to be." She looked down at the floor, as if she were a bit ashamed of something. "He's younger'n me, but he's been around. Has somethin' of a reputation. I don't know if what-all they say is true about him. But I love him, Raider. And he says he loves me."

"Don't they all."

She turned to slap him. Raider caught her hand and held her until she backed off. Then he apologized for having offended her. After all, she wasn't a whore anymore, but a seamstress.

Raider waited for a while before he started asking questions again. "What kind o' trouble is this boy in?"

"They say he killed somebody over in El Paso. A man named Pruitt, J. P. Pruitt. They say he shot him in the back."

"Pruitt a big man?"

She nodded. "One of them regular pillars of the community."

He chortled. "Your boy has t' go an' kill a town father."

"He didn't do it, damn it!"

"All right, all right," he said, trying to keep her calm. "If you say he didn't do it, he didn't do it."

"Well, he didn't! He was with me most of the night." She lowered her eyes. "They did find him standing over the body . . ."

"Sheeit."

"But I know he didn't do it! I never heard no shots. I was upstairs when Norris Hand came running out to arrest my boyfriend."

"Norris Hand?"

"The sheriff," Tillie said.

"And he was right there to nab your beau?"

She nodded. "They had him locked up ever since."

"An' you didn't hear any shots?"

She crossed her heart and raised her right hand. "I swear on my mama's grave that I never heard a single shot fired. My window was right there on the street. I saw 'em arrest Henry right on the spot."

"Henry, huh? Well, what makes you think I can get Henry sprung from jail?"

Tillie smiled sadly at him. "Oh, Raider. Soon as I heard there was a black-eyed cowboy at Madam Rosa's, I knew it had to be you. All the girls are talkin' about your big pecker. I knew you worked for Mr. Pinkerton. That's something like the law, ain't it?"

He sighed. "I ain't so sure I'm workin' in that line anymore. I didn't know it, but I had me a bellyfull of everybody else's trouble. From now on, I'm only concerned about *my* trouble."

She narrowed her expression, glaring at him. "That ain't like you, Raider. You ain't never been a man to be out just for yourself."

"I can't help this Henry," he insisted. "If they caught him standin' over the body..."

"He's innocent!" she cried. "And his name ain't Henry, not really. That's just his alias. Henry McCarty."

Raider smirked at her. "Oh yeah? What's his real name?"

"Bonney," she replied. "William H. Bonney."

Raider didn't have to think about that name. "Bonney's the one they call Billy the Kid! Hell, he's killed people."

"Not while he's been with me," Tillie replied.

"Honey, I can't..."

"Just go see him, Raider. Talk to him. Talk to the sheriff. I know you can help. I'll do anything." She touched his shoulder. "Anything."

He removed her hand. "You won't have t' do that, Tillie.

I'll go see 'im. But I can't promise I'll be any help."

"Thank you, Raider. I knew you'd do it. I knew you would."

He didn't tell her that he just wanted a chance to meet Billy the Kid.

NINE

For the first time in a month, Raider found himself thinking clearly. His main point of concern was getting in to see William H. Bonney, alias Henry McCarty, alias Billy the Kid. Of course, the local sheriff had no idea who he had in his jailhouse. Or did he? Maybe the whole thing had been a plan to take the Kid out of action. Wasn't Bonney in some trouble up in Lincoln County, New Mexico?

Raider tried to remember if the Pinkertons had been asked in for the six-gun square dance. It wasn't something the old man wanted to get into. Too bloody. But hell, this was Texas, not New Mexico.

The big man smiled as he guided Tillie's buggy over the border, trailing the knotty grey behind them. He was starting to think of himself as a detective again. Maybe he'd just take on the case of William Bonney himself, see if Tillie was telling the truth.

Hell, he hadn't been his ownself since he left Tucson. That wasn't him wrangling stray Mexican horses and cows, wasting all his time in a whorehouse, riding aimlessly toward an unknown destination. A man needed his work, plain and simple. He needed to keep on his toes, to stay sharp.

Tillie sat next to him on the buggy seat, glaring at him with her accusing blue eyes. "What are you lookin' so smug about?"

Raider smiled. "Just thinkin' of a way t' get in t' see your boy there."

Her face became tense with hope. "Oh, Raider, if you could do this for me I'd be beholdin' to you forever."

"I don't need forever," the big man replied. "I need your help now."

She put her hand on his forearm. "Name it."

"I want you t' make me a suit," he said, brushing her hand away. "I can't go t' see Bonney in this outfit. I don't want t' look like a trail bum when I face the sheriff."

Suddenly her hands were measuring his shoulders. "Oooh, darn you. You would have to be such a big hunk of a man."

"Trouble?"

"No, but it might take a while. I ain't never made a suit before."

Raider shook the reins, urging the harness-bred toward El Paso. That hadn't been him with Rodrigo, rounding up those horses. What kind of man did that for a living? Some poor bean-eater who wasn't sure where his next meal was coming from. Maybe chasing bad men was risky, but there was a certain dignity to it.

"Hey," Tillie said, "what are you doin'?"

Raider had turned the harness-bred away from El Paso's main thoroughfare.

He nodded over his shoulder. "Don't want t' attract no attention when I come in. You'll have t' show me the back way."

She bristled indignantly. "What makes you think I know the back way?"

"You always did."

So they came around the long route, sliding into a shadowed alley. It was still early, but the sun rendered a vivid purple glow over the city. After they had talked at Madam Rosa's Raider hadn't felt like sleeping, so they had set out immediately.

He reined back by a set of wooden stairs that went up to the second story of a flat-roofed plaster building. "You like livin' back here?" he asked.

Tillie shrugged. "It's quiet. And I just have to walk a few blocks to my work. Some kind of warehouse downstairs. I used to . . . well, let's just say I once had an intimate acquaintance with the owner."

Raider suddenly felt tired. "Listen, I'm gonna go up an' get some rest. You get started on that suit."

"I gotta measure you first."

Raider exhaled. "Okay, but make it quick."

"You're mighty bossy!"

He glared at her. "You want me to spring the Kid or not?"

That humbled her. They went upstairs to Tillie's place. It was small but tidy, the scent and colors belying a woman's touch. It reminded Raider of a cathouse.

Tillie wasted no time in taking the big man's measurements. "Maybe I can find a suit in town, but I doubt it. You're a damned big man."

When she measured his inseam, her hand lingered at his crotch. She reached for him and gave his cock a healthy squeeze. "Damn, you still got that muzzle-loader in your trousers."

Raider pushed her hand away. "What d'you think? That somebody cut it off?"

"I used to have a good time with that thing."

"I still do," the big man replied.

"How about now?" she offered.

He squinted at her. "Why?"

She shrugged. "I don't know. I reckon it'd be fun for me. And I'd feel less beholdin' to you, like we squared our accounts."

"The suit will do that."

"Why not, Raider? Why don't you want to do it with me? Am I ugly?"

He sighed. "No, honey, it ain't like that. I just spent a week at Madam Rosa's an' her girls like t' wore me out. And hell, you got that Kid. I thought you was in love with him."

She lowered her eyes. "I am."

"Ain't you doin' it with 'im?"

"Yeah," she replied without enthusiasm. "It ain't that important with us, though. It's all right, I mean, but it's bigger than that. And he ain't you, Raider. I love him, but I'd settle for you right now. It'd sure work out a few of the kinks."

Raider started to unbuckle his gunbelt. "I just want t' rest right now, Tillie. I got t' think, too, if I'm goin' in there t' see Bonney."

She frowned. "Can't you just go in like you are? Tell 'em you're Billy's cousin or somethin'?"

He hung the Colt on the bedpost. "See how much you know about these things? If I go in there lookin' like scum, sayin' I'm related t' the prisoner, they're gonna think I got a plan t' break 'im out. But if I go in there clean an' shaved an' lookin' like a dude, they got t' hear me out. See what I mean?"

"I reckon you know about those things."

She left him to sleep for a couple of hours.

When Raider woke up, she was there with the suit and a razor.

The big man nodded appreciatively. "Good job, honey."

She watched him as he cleaned up. "You're in luck. My boss had a suit she made for a man who didn't live to claim it. Shirts and tie, too. Want me to clean your boots?"

"That'd sure be a help."

He worked the razor as she shined his Justins.

"I want t' walk down t' the sheriff's office lookin' sharp. Let ever'body see the dude in the new suit. They'll know I'm somebody, or at least they'll suspect it."

Tillie dusted his Stetson while he put on the clothes.

"Hell, girl, perfect fit."

She helped him with the ribbon tie and stepped back to admire her work. "Not bad. You sure do look handsome."

He started to comb his hair and his mustache.

"You know, Raider, if you change your mind about gettin' on top of me, just let me know. I could sure use it."

He told her to wait until he was back from seeing William Bonney. She might not feel like it then, especially if there was no way for Raider to get her beau out of jail. Tillie replied that if anybody could spring William Bonney, Raider would be the one to do it.

High noon was the perfect time to walk down the main avenue. Everyone was on the run from the noontime heat, but that didn't stop them from noticing the long-striding, black-eyed, tall man in the new suit. *Somebody* had come to town, prompting the men to squint anxiously and the women to stare wide-eyed at the stranger.

Raider was hoping for something else, too. If it worked out right, he would be talking to William Bonney, alias Henry McCarty, in less than ten minutes. "'Scuse me," he said, tipping his hat to a storekeeper, "can you point me the way to Sheriff Hand's office?"

The speechless merchant gave a feeble indication of the direction.

Raider stepped up on the wooden sidewalk in front of the sign that declared: "Norris Hand, Sheriff and Justice of the Peace. And below it: "Town Jail of El Paso."

Raider thought it sort of vain to have a name take precedence over the jail. After all, sheriffs were shot and buried on a regular basis in border towns. It seemed to be asking for it to announce the name so boldly.

He pushed into the office without knocking.

A snoozing deputy was startled out of his siesta by the big man's entrance. He was a young man, stocky, with red hair and freckles. Big hands, rough knuckles that had seen some action busting heads. He glared at Raider with piercing green eyes. He looked to have a temper.

"Lookin' for Norris Hand," Raider said before the young man could speak.

"Sheriff ain't here," the young man replied.

Raider slammed his fist lightly into his hand, trying to look disappointed. He had been counting on the sheriff being absent for the noontime meal. He wanted to deal with a subordinate. It might be easier to wangle his way in to see the Kid.

"Wanted to speak to the sheriff hisself," Raider offered. "I reckon you can't be the one to help me though. Deputy . . . you got a name?"

"Bagget. Dub Bagget."

"Well, Mr. Bagget, I surely wish you could be of some assistance t' me, but I'm certain this kind o' thing would have t' be handled by the sheriff hisself and could not be the responsibility of someone not in charge."

Bagget frowned, taking the bait like a hungry catfish. "When the sheriff ain't here, I *am* in charge, partner. You got a name?"

Raider extended his hand. "Name's Raider. Pinkerton operative."

Bagget shook hands with him. The young deputy had a good grip. Strong and mean. Not somebody you wanted to cross unless you were looking for a fight.

"Pinkerton, huh?"

Raider stayed on cue, pulling out his credentials for a once-over by the deputy. "I'm here about the McCarty boy."

Bagget glanced up with those hostile green eyes. "What about the McCarty boy? Huh?"

The big man from Arkansas just grinned like a possum. "Look here, sonny boy, I knowed you wouldn't be able t' handle this." He took his credentials from Bagget's hands. "I'll come back when your daddy is home. This kind o' bus'ness oughta be done between growed men, anyway."

"Why do you want to see McCarty?" Bagget insisted.

Putting the credentials inside his coat, Raider replied, "I ain't sure it's somethin' I should talk 'bout with you, Dub. You'll find out soon enough."

The deputy's face darkened. "Now look here, Pinkerton. You just say what you come to say. I can hear it as well as the sheriff."

Raider exhaled. "You sure I can trust you?"

He pointed to his badge, a tin star. "I'm law, just like the sheriff. If this concerns that McCarty boy, it concerns me."

"Okay, but I hope you don't get us both in trouble."

"Say it, Pinkerton."

Raider told him that it wasn't much really, just that somebody had hired him to look into the fact of McCarty's guilt or innocence. That somebody did not believe that McCarty had killed Mr. Pruitt and was willing to pay him to try to prove it. Of course, Raider went on in a patronizing tone, he didn't for one minute doubt the competence of the El Paso law, but he had to ask McCarty some questions just to get a few things straight. After all, he was only earning his keep like everyone else.

"I'll come back when Hand is here," Raider said finally. "He prob'bly wouldn't like it if you let me in t' see McCarty. Wouldn't want you steppin' over no lines of authority or nothin'."

Bagget stood up behind the desk where he had been sleeping. "Now hold on, Pinkerton. You can see McCarty now. Course, I got to search you first, make sure you ain't carryin' no guns or knives."

Raider consented to a thorough search and even urged Bagget to stand at the door that opened into the jail area. He wanted him to watch the whole thing. Cover him while he talked to McCarty.

"You never know what one like that is gonna try," Raider said.

Bagget had to agree. "I'll be right behind you, partner.

Don't fret. If McCarty tries anything, I'll plug him."

With that said, he opened a drawer in the desk and took out the keys to the cell room in back of the office. He opened the door and admitted Raider into the musty enclosure. Raider glanced toward the four alcoves that were framed by sets of iron bars.

"Just built these new cells," Bagget said proudly. "They're all empty 'cept the one holdin' McCarty. Hey, Henry, you got a visitor."

Raider peered into the shadows, watching as Billy the Kid stepped up to the bars to stare back at him.

The Kid's face was by no means hard or rugged. He looked sort of like the type of boy that Raider had seen employed in telegraph offices as a clerk. Brownish hair, thin mustache and fuzz beard, lanky arms and legs. But there was something in the eyes that didn't fit—a glassy quality, a lack of focus that made the Kid seem to be looking at something else, when in reality he was looking straight at you.

"I don't know this yahoo," the Kid said. "Tell him to get the hell out of here."

"He's a Pinkerton," Bagget replied. "Said somebody hired him to prove you's innocent, even though we all know better."

Bagget laughed, expecting Raider to join in.

The big man had locked eyes with the Kid. "He's right. I'm a Pinkerton, come t' help you."

"Shit!" the Kid said, chortling. "No Pinkerton ever helped a man like me. They're just trouble."

"Tillie sent me."

Bonney's face slacked. "All right, I'll talk to him."

Raider cast a glance at Bagget. "Don't get too far away."

"I ain't goin' nowhere, Pink-man."

Raider stepped over next to the bars. He leaned in, smiling. "Hello, Billy," he said in a low voice.

Bonney scowled at him. "You know. Tillie told you."

Raider nodded, thinking he had never seen such a tender-looking youth with such a bad reputation. Bonney had supposedly killed quite a few men in his time. But hell, the Kid didn't look much older than twenty.

"So you come to take me back to New Mexico?" Bonney asked through clenched teeth. "Take me back to the prison I run away from? Well, you're too late, Hoss. They're gonna hang me right here for somethin' I didn't do."

Raider looked back at Bagget, shaking his head, smirking. Then, to the Kid: "Look, Tillie says you didn't do it, kill that Pruitt I mean."

Bonney laughed. "Don't that beat all. Listen, big man, I planted my share. I killed my first man when I was seventeen. And I killed a few since then. But I didn't kill this one. And they're gonna hang me for it. Don't that just tickle your spiskets?"

"You'll get a trial."

"Yeah," Bonney chortled, "and then I'll get the noose."

Raider found himself being swayed by the Kid. But he did not want to be taken in by a sob story. He needed proof.

"Where were you the night Pruitt was killed?"

Bonney shrugged. "With Tillie. I been hangin' with her since I met her. Takin' me a little break since I went on the lam. El Paso's usually a good place to lay low, least I heard it was."

"Used t' be," Raider replied. "Too many solid citizens these days."

Bonney pushed his face against the bars. "Who sent you, big man? Are you from the Regulators? Huh? Tell me who you really are!"

"Just who I say I am," Raider said. "I ain't from Lincoln County, boy."

Bonney eyed him suspiciously. "What do you know about Lincoln County?"

Raider shrugged. "I know some. You were mixed up with some land barons up that way. Cattlemen. You rode with the Regulators. I heard you caused some trouble up at Blazer's Mill."

The Kid smiled. "Yeah, you're a Pinkerton, all right. I always wondered why nobody ever hired y'all to mix it up with us Regulators."

"We ain't stupid," the big man replied.

Bonney shook his head defeatedly. "I reckon you think I shot Pruitt just like the rest of 'em."

"Maybe. But maybe what Tillie said was true."

"And what'd she say?" the Kid asked.

"That you was framed. That you was with her all night and

that she never heard a gunshot. That you was standin' over the body when they caught you. But she said you didn't do it."

Bonney shook a finger at him, waving excitedly. "That's it! That's the way it happened. I never killed that man. I swear it. Hell, why would I lie? They're gonna hang me anyway. Only I ain't gonna give 'em the pleasure of hangin' Billy the Kid. They're gonna hang Henry McCarty."

Raider grimaced. "We'll see, boy. But I'm gonna look into it."

Bonney frowned. "And it don't bother you that I'm in trouble up to Lincoln County?"

"This ain't New Mexico, kid. This is Texas . . ."

"You're damned right it's Texas," came a booming voice from behind them. "El Paso, Texas. And I'm the law here. Bagget, what's this man doin' talkin' to the prisoner?"

Raider turned to look at a sturdy, grey-haired man standing in the doorway. "You must be Norris Hand."

"He's a Pinkerton, Sheriff," Bagget declared.

"Come to set me free," Billy the Kid chimed in.

Raider glared back at Bonney. "Sit tight, boy. Don't blow it. That stuff in Lincoln County don't mean nothin' t' me. You keep your head an' you might just get out o' this thing alive."

"Into my office," ordered Norris Hand.

Raider figured the best thing to do would be to obey him.

Norris Hand was fuming. When he took off his wide-brimmed Stetson, Raider saw the top of his head was salt and pepper. Maybe he wasn't as old as he appeared at first. Sun-browned face, clear brown eyes. The kind of man you might hire to ramrod a cattle company for a trail drive. He'd be severe but fair and do everything by the book, never deviating from the rules, at least on the surface. A man like Norris Hand would never let you know what he was really thinking or doing, unless he had a good reason for revealing himself.

Raider tried to stay happy. "Mind if I take a seat?" he asked as Hand went behind the desk to hang up his Stetson.

The sheriff turned back quickly, glaring at the big Pinkerton. "You can stay standin', partner. 'Cause you ain't gonna be around here long enough to get comfortable."

Dub Bagget wanted to get in on the act. "He's a Pinkerton,

heriff. He's been hired to prove McCarty innocent."

Hand scowled at his deputy. "He talked his way past you retty easy, Dub. Maybe I need me a deputy who ain't so easy o fool."

"Hey," Bagget said, wounded. "He didn't fool nobody."

Raider shrugged, trying to play the reasonable party. "He's ight, Mr. Hand. I am a Pinkerton. I have been hired to look nto McCarty's case."

"Get out of here, Dub," the sheriff said to his subordinate.

"But Mr. Hand . . ."

"Git!"

Bagget turned to go, pointing a finger at Raider. "You bet-er tell him you didn't fool me, Pinkerton. You better."

Hand raised his voice. "Git the devil out of here, Dub!"

Bagget stormed out, his face flushed.

"He just let me in t' see my client," Raider offered. "You voulda done the same thing."

Hand glared at him. "I would?"

Raider nodded, sitting in a wooden chair. "Yep, I'm 'fraid ou'd have t', Sheriff. That boy in there has some rights until e's proved guilty."

"You a lawyer?" Hand grunted.

"I'm a Pinkerton, sir. I been hired t' look into the case of Henry McCarty by a innerested party."

Hand laughed sarcastically. "That whore? Where'd she get nough money to hire a Pink?"

Raider's black eyes narrowed a little, switching from smile o frown. "She's a seamstress, Hand."

"She's a whore anyway, you . . ."

Raider leaned forward. "You know, Hand, you're right hort on manners. Now I come in here real polite-like t' find ut what I needed t' know. I admit I softsoaped your deputy a ittle, but he followed procedure. He patted me down and he vas watchin' us from the start. Any problems with the story o far?"

Hand calmed down some, but he still didn't like Raider eing there. "This case is closed, partner. We found McCarty tandin' over the body."

"Convenient, if you ask me," Raider said.

"Nobody asked you."

Raider leaned back in the chair. "So you wouldn't mind if went down t' that section o' town an' asked a few questions Or maybe visit the widow Pruitt and ask her a few questions?

"Stay out of my town, boy."

"I'll be happy t' stay away from your town if you just sho me proof that you investigated the killin' o' this Pruitt, Raider replied. "I got one witness who says she didn't hear single shot fired."

Hand grinned hatefully. "That woman is McCarty' whore," he said with a tone of victory. "She'd say anything t get him freed."

The big man shrugged. "Okay, nobody can doubt that."

"Huh?" Hand wasn't sure he had heard right.

"I'm willin' to go along with the river if it's flowin' in th right direction, Sheriff. You're correct when you say tha whore would say anything. But did you ask anybody else i the neighborhood if they heard shots?"

Hand pointed a finger at him. "I don't have to tell yo nothin', Pink."

"And how was you there so quick, pickin' up Bonn . . McCarty when he just happened to be standin' over th body?"

"None of your damned business!"

Raider shook his head back and forth, slowly trying t consider the possibilities. "Yes, sir, Sheriff Hand, you left few holes in this case. Less'n you want t' tell me what yo really found out."

Hand seemed to draw back, smiling slightly, his eyes nar rowed. "I don't have to tell you nothin', Pink. Hell, how do even know you are who you say you are?"

Raider reached into his coat. "I got me a credential."

"Credentials can be bogus."

"Okay," the big man said, conceding to the logical trail "why don't you just wire the Pinkerton National Detectiv Agency, Chicago, Illinois? Ask Mr. William Wagner if h knows who I am. Then tell him I'm takin' McCarty's case o behalf o' Miss Tillie Creighton. Think you can remember al that?"

Hand leered at him over the desk. "I might just do that, bi

man. And you better be tellin' the truth or you'll be sittin' in there with McCarty."

Raider stood up. "I'm somebody you got t' live with, Hand. I can be your friend or your enemy. If you really want t' get t' the truth, you'll be my friend."

"Get out," Hand replied. "And watch your step, boy. First time you land in trouble, I'm herdin' you into one of them cells. If you do somethin' wrong in my town, I'll walk all over you."

"Pretty long walk," Raider said.

Norris Hand pointed toward the door. "Like I said, you better not make no trouble. Or you'll go on trial with the boy in there."

"I'll be seein' you, Norris."

"Not if I see you first."

Raider went out, slamming the door behind him. He wondered if Hand had been hiding something. Maybe the sheriff was just plain ornery by nature. The big man couldn't blame him for not wanting outside interference in a pending case where man had not yet come to the trial. But as far as the big man could see, there really *were* a few unanswered questions about the murder of the man named Pruitt. Raider just needed to find somebody to talk, to help with a few facts.

As he stepped off the sidewalk into the street, he heard the voice as it rolled through the dust. "Pinkerton!"

He turned to his left to see Dub Bagget standing there with his hand hanging over a bone-handled Peacemaker. "You made a fool out of me, Pinkerton," Bagget said, his hand itchy near the butt of the Colt.

Raider opened his coat, "I ain't packin', Dub. But hell, you shoulda knowed that. You patted me down. And I told your boss you did right."

Bagget shook his head. "That don't make whiskey, partner. You may not have guns, but you got two fists."

He tried to grin at the red-faced deputy. "Dub, if you an' me was t' fight, that sheriff'll run me in an' lock me up."

Bagget smiled. "You chicken? Huh?"

Raider was beginning to lose his composure. The whole thing with Hand had left him on edge. Maybe what he needed was a good fight.

"I ain't chicken, Dub. What say we find a place where there ain't no witnesses and mix it up good."

Bagget's smile left his round face. "Just you and me?"

"Unless you're chicken."

"Come on, Pinkerton, I'm gonna whup your ass."

They fell into stride and started for the edge of town.

TEN

They toed the line in an empty corral at the outskirts of town. There were no spectators beyond the birds that circled overhead in the hot afternoon breeze. Raider had stripped to the waist so as not to dirty his new clothes. Deputy Bagget kept on his shirt and his hat, only taking off his sidearm to hang it on the corral fence.

When their feet hit the line, Raider swung first, catching Bagget in the hard part of his head. The big man's fist stung with the blow. Bagget just grunted, not seeming to feel the punch at all. He came on strong, rushing Raider with a volley of hard lefts and rights.

Raider tried to cover up, but some of the blows got through. He knew by the scars on Bagget's knuckles that the deputy could fight. But he also figured that Bagget's fights always ended quickly, with one or two strong punches from the deputy taking out some drunk, rowdy cowboy who would spend the night in jail.

As the blows came in on him, Raider tried to hold his own, using his knowledge to slip the lefts and rights, waiting for the fight to progress.

A contest had many stages, the big man knew. Bagget was strong at the beginning, able to keep his arms up as he swung. But the more he flailed at Raider, the heavier his hands became. And while he did some damage to the big man's body, Raider could feel the punches weakening as the fight progressed.

"Gonna kill you," Bagget grunted, trying to redouble his efforts.

But the zip just wasn't there. Bagget stepped back, breathing hard, trying to suck air into his lungs. Raider straightened up and came on, firing a roundhouse left hook that caught

Bagget in the soft roll of flab over his belly. The deputy grunted again, going down to one knee.

"You finished?" Raider offered, giving him a chance to concede.

Bagget staggered to his feet. "I'll give you finished!"

He rushed headlong at Raider, who side-stepped and tripped him as he ran by. Bagget fell flat on his face. Raider somehow didn't feel angry enough to attack the man while he was down.

"Come on, lawman. Admit you can't beat me."

Bagget wheeled around, turning over on the ground. His hand whipped forward, launching a projectile at Raider. The small rock caught Raider on the forehead, stinging him but not doing much damage. It only served to make him bull-mad.

"Chuckin' rocks, huh! Get on your feet you bag o' guts."

The deputy managed to stand up. "You tripped, Pinkerton. If you can trip me, I can throw a rock."

Raider let his fists reply. He stalked Bagget, flipping the left at the man's chin. Bagget tried to fend off the blows, but he was arm weary and could only retreat. Raider backed him into the corral fence, going wild, slamming hard punches in Bagget's face and torso.

The deputy finally slumped to the ground. His face was bleeding. Raider shuddered, stepping back to look at the beaten lawman.

"Don't kill me," Bagget said.

Raider's black eyes focused on the man's swollen countenance. "You pushed it, Bagget. I never wanted t' hurt anyone. You just pissed me off when you hit me with that rock."

Bagget held up his hands. "No more. I done had enough."

Raider reached down to help the man to his feet.

Bagget took the big man's hand, but he did not get up. Instead, he swung a leg into Raider's groin, catching him squarely in the privates. Raider grunted and went down to the ground, feeling nauseous.

The deputy tried to come after him again, throwing punches that were weak and misdirected. Raider rolled away, wishing the pain in his craw would go away. The sneaky son of a bitch had caught him off guard with that low blow.

Raider hit the edge of the corral and pulled himself to his feet.

Bagget was also standing, his hands raised. "You had enough, Pinkerton?"

Raider sucked air into his lungs. He felt a surge of strength in his body. He charged Bagget, buffeting him to the ground. When the deputy tried to get up, Raider applied the tip of his Justin boot to the man's chin.

Bagget's head snapped back. He fell on the ground, quivering. For a second, Raider thought the deputy might die in a twitching spasm. But Bagget seemed to catch his wind and he started to sit up.

Raider moved to kick him again.

Bagget cringed, falling back on the ground. "No more. I mean it. I had enough."

"'Scuse me if I don't help you up this time."

Raider turned away and started for the corral fence where his clothes were hanging. Tillie would be mad that his pants were ripped and dirty. At least he hadn't torn up the coat and the fancy shirt.

"Pinkerton!"

He looked around to see Dub Bagget with the Colt in his hand.

"I ain't packin'," Raider said again. "If you shoot me, it'll be cold blooded murder. Not t' mention the fact that you'd be considered a poor loser."

Bagget's face was a bloody mess. He spoke through swollen lips. "I'm takin' you in, Pinkerton. For fighting."

Raider laughed. "So, it was a trick after all. You really didn't challenge me. You just wanted me t' do somethin' I could be taken t' jail for."

The deputy frowned. "It ain't like that."

"Oh, I see. You're just runnin' me in because you can't stand t' lose a fight. That it?"

He was confused. "You fought. You broke the law."

Raider gestured all around him. "Come on, Dub. Take a look. Ain't nobody saw us fight. You need witnesses."

"You're all bloody!"

"So are you," the big man replied. "Course, my story might be a little differ'nt than yours. And it don't matter in a court o' law, cause it'd be my word 'gainst yours. Hell, I might even tell the truth. Admit t' fightin' but tell how you provoked me. How's that gonna look t' Sheriff Hand?"

Bagget's gunhand was trembling. "I'm warnin' you, Pinkerton."

Raider's black eyes narrowed. "You can shoot me, Dub. But as far as I can see, there's somethin' goin' on in El Paso. Somethin' t' do with that kid you got in the jail."

The deputy thumbed back the hammer of the Colt. "You're lyin', Pink-man. Sheriff caught McCarty red-handed. Standin' over the body of Mr. Pruitt."

"Then help me prove that," Raider offered. "Unless you're afraid the truth might upset the horse cart."

"Nobody's afraid of the truth in El Paso!" Bagget cried.

Raider started walking, keeping Bagget in the corner of his eye. "Then you ain't gonna shoot me, deputy. You're gonna let me go 'bout my bus'ness. You won't shoot an innocent man, even if he did just whip your ass."

Bagget raised the Colt. "Don't take another step!"

But Raider's back was turned to him now. "Go on," he challenged. "Plug me in the back. There'll just be somebody else here when I don't turn up. You can't hide the truth forever, Dub."

"Pinkerton!"

But Raider kept on, heading back into town. He expected the Colt to explode any second, calling his bluff. But he turned out to be right on this one. Bagget didn't shoot him. Maybe the deputy wanted to know the truth as much as he did.

"Good Lord, Raider, what happened to you?"

The big man stood in Tillie's doorway, his coat and shirt in hand. "Had me a little fight with the deputy."

"Bagget?"

He nodded.

Tillie touched his face, examining the wounds. Women seemed to like to look at wounds. They were always studying a way to make them better.

"Not bad," she said. "How do you feel?"

He shrugged. "Shaky. That bastard kicked me in the nuts."

"You get the best of him?"

Raider chuckled. "I'd say we got the best of each other. Although I was standin' at the end."

She took his arm. "Come on, sit down. Good Lord, look at those pants. I'll have to clean them and mend them."

"Sorry."

He sat down on the edge of her bed.

Tillie doctored his cuts and bruises, applying a wet towel and then some sort of tincture that burned like the devil. "You see Billy?" she asked.

Raider nodded. "I did."

"How is he?"

The big man shrugged. "All right, I reckon. You know he's also in trouble up New Mexico way."

Tillie sighed. "Yeah, I know. But I'd hoped me and him could hook up here and he could live under his other name."

"I don't know, Tillie."

She frowned. "What's wrong?"

"I seen his type before," Raider replied. "Oh, he's a good enough ol' boy, I'm sure. But . . ."

"But what?"

He exhaled. "I don't know, Tillie. I just get a feelin' when I look at 'im. Like he ain't all there."

"You don't know him like I do."

Raider shook his head. "I gotta be wary 'bout a kid that so easily admits he's killed people."

Tillie gaped at him. "Did he say he killed Pruitt?"

"No, that's the one he says he didn't do. And you know somethin'? I believe 'im. I really do."

"Oh, Raider, if you could just prove he didn't kill Pruitt."

"I'm gonna try, Tillie. I'm sure as hell gonna try. Oww . . ."

He still felt the pain in his craw.

Tillie, who now seemed overjoyed, stood up. "Get them pants off. I got to clean and patch them before the dirt sets in."

Raider obeyed without thinking. He was not modest about taking off his pants in front of Tillie. After all, she had seen him naked before. And the way he felt, there was little chance of anything happening between them.

Tillie grimaced at his boots. "Look at that. After I spent all that time polishing them for you."

Raider stretched out on the bed, feeling his aches and pains.

After a few moments, Tillie was standing over him again. "Here," she said, "let me see if he hurt you."

"What?"

"You said he hit you in the balls."

"Yeah."

She started to tug at his underwear. "Well then, let me have a look. Maybe I can make them feel better."

It was useless to protest. If Tillie wanted to give him an inspection, he would not resist. Besides, with the dull ache in his groin, he doubted that she could get him hard.

Her slender fingers fondled his scrotum, gently turning his cock and balls in her hand. "How's that feel?" she asked.

Raider grunted. "Don't hurt as bad as it should."

"Let me kiss 'em and make 'em better."

"Tillie!"

But her mouth was at work, sliding over his privates, wet lips and tongue on his skin.

But his prick did not spring to life.

"He really musta kicked you hard," Tillie said. "Maybe a cold cloth."

She went to the pump, wetting a washrag. When she came back, Raider saw that she had bared her breasts. He started to say something, until she swabbed his crotch with the cold cloth. He had to admit that it took some of the pain away. But still no erection.

"Give up, Tillie. It ain't gonna work. I got kicked square in the stones. It might be a while before . . . oww . . ."

She rolled his balls in the cloth. "We'll see, cowboy. I ain't forgot all the tricks of my former trade."

Her tongue lolled around the head of his prick while she worked on his scrotum with the cloth.

But his shaft remained limp.

"Don't fight it," she whispered. "It'll feel a whole lot better if it gets hard. Just let go."

She hovered over him, taking his cock between her soft breasts. Raider grunted as he felt the swelling between his legs. Tillie had always been a good whore, full of tricks that could get any man rigid.

"Goodness," she teased. "You're not hurt as bad as you thought."

He glared at her. "What if the Kid finds out about this? He'll want t' kill me."

"Then I won't tell him," Tillie replied. "Unless you don't give me what I want. And you know what that is."

His cock was in her hand, fully erect and ready.

"Damn you, woman."

She came up onto the bed, straddling him, hiking up her dress. She closed her eyes as she searched for the opening of her cunt, guiding the prickhead to the wetness of her font. Her hips began their slow descent, taking him in, filling her with his length.

"That thing's so big," she said through her clenched teeth.

Raider watched her, wondering if he could stand the pain. Despite her efforts, there was still a dull aching in his groin. Tillie had no intention of letting him go now that she had him inside her.

"You okay?" she moaned, looking down at him.

He nodded. "Don't know if I'll be able to make it spit, though."

"I'll make it spit, honey. You just hold on."

Her hips worked up and down, driving him toward a release. When he came, she collapsed on top of him, rubbing her chest in his face. Raider groaned, aware of the bruises on his torso.

"I'm sorry," she said, touching his lips. "Here, let me tend you."

She wet the cloth again and washed his whole body.

Raider had to admit that her ministrations made him feel better.

Tillie put her head between his legs. "Ooh, look at this bruise on the inside of your thigh. That's where he kicked you. He just grazed your balls. You ain't hurt bad at all."

She probably would have started up again, but Raider told her to go make dinner. He closed his eyes, drifting off for a while. When she woke him, he smelled stew, but he also felt Tillie's nervousness.

"What is it?" he asked.

She pointed toward the door. "I thought I heard somebody outside. It's gettin' dark. I thought I heard footsteps on the stairs."

Raider eased out of the bed, still feeling the effects of the fight. He grabbed his Colt and stepped toward the door. The heavy knocking on the door caused him to thumb the hammer of the Peacemaker.

He nodded to Tillie. "See who it is."

She slid next to the threshold. "Who's knockin' on my door?"

"It's Bagget. I'm lookin' for the Pinkerton."

Raider nodded for her to open the door. When Bagget came in, Raider knocked him to the floor and put the gun in his face. The wide-eyed deputy gaped up at him.

"Don't kill me, mister."

Raider held steady with the Peacemaker. "What are you doin' here, deputy?"

"I come to help," he replied. "I was thinkin' about what you said and I want to help. I want to help you find out the truth."

"Shit," the big man scowled, "why would you do that? Why would you go 'gainst the sheriff?"

"I don't want to go against the sheriff," Bagget replied. "It's just that . . . well, you . . ."

"Go on."

The deputy sighed. "You fight like a man who thinks he's right."

Raider eased off on the hammer of the Peacemaker. "You sure this ain't some kinda trap?"

"I don't blame you for not trustin' me, big man. But you whupped my ass. And if I had wanted you dead, I'd have plugged you back there at the corral."

A chortle from the tall, Arkansas man. "Yeah, I reckon you would."

"I can show you everything," Bagget insisted. "I can tell you all the facts of the case. We can go right now."

Raider pulled the man to his feet. "No. Tomorrow, first thing in the mornin'."

Bagget nodded. "Okay. Whatever you say."

The deputy started for the door. "See you at sunup, Pinkman."

"Name's Raider."

"Raider."

"And Bagget . . ."

The deputy turned to look at him. "What?"

"No bullshit. Comprende?"

"Comprende."

Bagget left them, trudging down the stairs.

"Looks like you beat him up pretty good," Tillie offered.

The big man grunted. "I just hope he ain't plannin' t' bushwhack me."

Tillie touched his face. "What was all that about the corral?"

"Never mind," he replied, turning away. "Just dish up some o' that stew. I'm hungry as hell."

When they had eaten, they went back to bed. Raider told her not to get her hopes up, but Tillie had other ideas. She went to work and kept him up the better part of the night, using him until she had had her fill.

Raider waited in the early hours of morning, watching the alley from the roof of the building next to Tillie's place. He heard the clicking of boot heels from the sidewalk on the main street. The echoes carried for a long time in the stillness of a sleeping town. A man turned off the street, into the alley that approached the stairs to Tillie's.

It was Bagget, striding slowly down the alley. Raider studied him for the telltale signs of a man anticipating an ambush—nervousness, looking behind him, watching the shadows. But Bagget just walked trustingly down the alley to keep his appointment. Raider looked beyond the deputy, trying to spot anyone that might have come with him. He seemed to be alone.

Bagget started up the steps to Tillie's door.

Raider rattled the lever of his Winchester.

Bagget glanced up at the big man from Arkansas. "Raider?"

"Just takin' a few precautions, Bagget. Meet me on the other side o' this warehouse."

Raider ran across the rooftop, shinnying down a rain gutter at the corner of the structure.

Bagget came around the corner with his hand on his Colt.

"No need to worry, Dub. I ain't gonna double-cross you. You said you wanted t' help; now's your chance."

Bagget nodded. "Okay, what you want me to do?"

Raider leaned back against the wall of the building. "Well, you can start by tellin' me how the sheriff came to catch McCarty standin' over the body o' that man Pruitt."

The deputy's eyes narrowed. "Don't know if I ought to . . ."

"Then you don't really want t' help, do you? You just want t' waste my time. Forget it, Dub. I can find out what I need t' know on my own."

"Wait." Bagget exhaled defeatedly. "All right. Mr. Hand got a message to come to the alley where the body was found."

"From who?"

"Nobody knows," Dub replied. "It was left on the door at the sheriff's house. At least that's what he told me."

"Where was this alley?" Raider asked.

Bagget pointed back toward Tillie's place. "Right over there. Where I just come from."

Raider started for the alley. "Come on, I want t' see first-hand."

Bagget told him how the body was found, lying facedown with a hole in the back. "A big hole," Bagget said, measuring with his hands.

The big man scoffed. "Hell, boy, that hole is as big as a cat's head."

The deputy shrugged. "I know what I saw."

Raider shook his head. "Then a wound that size woulda had t' be made by a scattergun, or a cannon."

"Come to think of it, it did kind of look like the same wound old Mose Henshaw had when his old lady plugged him at close range with a scattergun. I never thought about it before."

Raider eyed him accusingly. "An' what kind of gun was Bonn . . . McCarty carryin' when you picked 'im up?"

"Colt .36," Bagget replied. "An old Navy. He bought it right here in town. Or so he said."

"No scattergun?" Raider offered.

Bagget's face showed his bewilderment. "No."

"Then McCarty couldn'ta killed 'im."

Bagget had to think before he could come up with an explanation. "He could have shot him a bunch of times with that Navy."

Raider shook his head again. "Tillie swears she didn't hear no shots. If McCarty had opened up with that pistol, he woulda been heard. Same if he used a scattergun. Even if he had enough time t' shoot the scattergun an' then hide it, he still woulda been heard."

Bagget lowered his head. "Listen, I was thinkin' about that. So last night after you threw me out, I went around to a few places back here, you know, where people sleep sometimes."

"I'm listenin'."

The deputy sighed, like he was having trouble getting it out. "Well, I asked old Dell Peters—he's a rummy hangs out in these alleys—anyways, I asked him if he heard anything that night. He had a hard time rememberin', but he finally recalled somethin' 'cause it was so unusual. Seems that night, when Mr. Pruitt was killed, Dell heard a wagon back here. Chugged to a stop right about here and then somethin' hit the ground. Wagon just went on. Next thing you know, Dell heard shoutin'. Looked out to see the commotion."

"Wonder why he didn't come forward?" Raider asked.

"Nobody'd believe him," Bagget replied. "He's just a rummy."

"But that'd be two witnesses. Did you ask this Peters if he heard any shots?"

"Said he didn't. And he would have too. He was sleepin' in that loft yonder. He would've heard it."

Raider hunkered down, looking at the ground. "So Pruitt was killed an' then dumped here. Somebody notified the sheriff an' he came lookin'. Poor Billy was just in the wrong place at the wrong time."

Bagget's brow wrinkled. "Who's Billy?"

"Oh, I meant Henry," Raider replied, trying to cover his slip of thc tongue. "I used t' work with a boy named Billy McCarty. I guess I got them two confused."

"Yeah, I reckon. You really think McCarty is innocent?"

Raider shrugged. "Well, he sure as hell didn't shoot Pruitt in this alley with a scattergun. And we have one more question t' answer, which is maybe the most important one. Why would McCarty want t' kill Pruitt in the first place? Did they know each other?"

"I reckon not."

Raider stood up, glancing at the sky. "Gettin' t' be hot. What time your boss show up in the mornin'?"

"'Bout seven," Bagget replied. "Why?"

"Wouldn't mind takin' a look at McCarty's Colt. See if it was even fired. Y' think you could swing it?"

Bagget nodded. "One thing first. I think you ought to know."

"What's that?"

"Well, I had my suspicions about this whole thing from the first," the deputy said. "Only I didn't have nobody to talk to. That's why I had to come see you after we fought. Like I said, you fought like somebody who believed he was right."

"Get t' the point, boy."

Bagget sighed. "Just this. Mr. Pruitt, the man who was killed, was married to Norris Hand's sister Thelma. Now Mr. Pruitt was known to have some wealth. And as his sole kin, Thelma gets it all."

Raider studied the young man. He was shaking, like he had betrayed his commander in combat. It had taken a lot for the deputy to come right out and say it.

"You think Sheriff Hand stood t' gain by Pruitt's death?"

Bagget shook his head, almost in tears. "I don't know, Raider. I just keep thinkin' that I'd rather have a rich sister than a poor one."

"Well, I may just go talk t' this Thelma," the big man replied. "But right now you gotta get me in t' have a look at McCarty's weapon. And if worse comes to worse, we may have t' dig up the body of Mr. Pruitt, or at least talk t' the undertaker 'bout that wound in 'is back."

Bagget led the way to the jailhouse.

Raider was examining the Colt when Norris Hand walked in. Good, the big man thought, now he could force a showdown. Billy's gun hadn't even been fired. All six chambers were primed.

"You're just the man I want t' see," Raider said. "I got evidence you should be int'rested in. If you can . . ."

Norris Hand grabbed a scattergun from the wall rack and leveled it at Raider. "Don't move," the sheriff ordered. "You're under arrest."

Raider gawked at the lawman. "What the hell?"

"Listen to him, Mr. Hand," the deputy urged. "He knows what he's talkin' about."

Hand unfolded a telegram and tossed it to Raider. "I been told to detain you, big man. Your man Wagner sent the request after I wired him to check on you. Seems he's coming here himself to get you. You're in a bunch of trouble, honcho."

Raider eyed the telegram, wondering if it was genuine. 'What kind o' trouble?"

"Somethin' about horses in Tucson. Says it all right there. ust come in."

Raider felt the sinking in his gut. The whole thing with the iorses had been so innocent. Somebody must have com- ·lained to give Wagner the wrong idea. Hell, it probably ıadn't looked too good with him throwing all that back pay round down in Nogales. Now Wagner was coming in person ɔ check up on him. He had to take that as a good sign, specially since it was the only good sign he had.

"Come on, big man," Hand said, waving the shotgun.

"You gotta listen to him, Sheriff," Dub Bagget said, trying ɔ intercede. "He makes a lot of sense."

Hand glared at his deputy. "I'll deal with you later, boy. ℓight now I got to get this one behind bars. Now lift that Colt ·ut of your holster real slow-like and drop it on the desk."

Raider had two choices. Try to run or wait for Wagner. If e ran, he would surely look guilty. If he stayed, Norris Hand night kill him

"I want a piece o' paper an' a pencil afore I go," Raider aid.

Hand squinted at him. "For what?"

"I'm gonna write a letter," the big man replied. "I want t' vrite t' my old pardner, Doc Weatherbee. I want t' tell 'im ıat if I turn up dead, he's t' come lookin' for you, Hand. He's ı Chicago. But he'd come to avenge me."

"And if I don't give you the paper?" the sheriff asked.

Raider smiled. "Then you kill me with the shotgun, but not efore I kill you with my Peacemaker."

Hand hesitated, but then told Bagget to supply Raider with vhat he wanted. Before he started writing, Raider told the eputy to go get Tillie. He was finishing the letter as Bagget shered her into the office.

"Go mail this, Tillie," the big man said. "No, you don't go vith her, Bagget. She goes alone. Then, when she comes ack, I'll give myself up."

Tillie went to mail the letter. Raider had really addressed it ɔ one of the clerks at the Pinkerton Agency, a man named imson. He had only used the street address, not the name of the agency, just in case Hand went down to the post office later to intercept it.

When Tillie came back, Raider lifted his Colt and put it on the table. "Lock me up, Hand. But don't get too cocky. If Wagner's comin', he'll bail me out."

They ushered him back to the cell room. William Bonney was hanging on the bars of his cell. He laughed when he saw Raider.

"I knew they'd lock up anybody who came to help me," the Kid said.

Then he saw Tillie and he began to cry her name. Tillie started to run to him, but Bagget restrained her. Tears were rolling down her cheeks.

"I love you!" she cried. "I'll never rest till you're free."

Raider was tempted to make a move in all the commotion, but Hand was too close with the scattergun. Could it have been the same gun used to kill the man named Pruitt? He stepped into the cell, hearing the metallic clang as the door was shut and locked.

"Worst sound in the world, ain't it?" Billy the Kid said to him.

Raider had to agree that it was.

ELEVEN

Raider hadn't been in jail much. He had been locked up a few times, he had even been captured by some of his adversaries and held for days on end. But most of the time it had been different. He had usually been bailed out right away, or was just sleeping off a drunk. He'd pay the fine the next morning and leave town with his tail between his legs. Lawmen were usually good to him, as he had assisted them many times. A Pink's reputation went a long way toward keeping him out of trouble, at least it had in the past.

Now he was locked up in Norris Hand's El Paso jail, waiting for Wagner. It nearly drove him crazy the first week, just sitting, listening to Bonney talk. He wasn't even sure when Wagner would get there. Maybe Norris Hand's telegram had been a fake. No, he wouldn't have known about the horse ranchers in Tucson. Looking back, Raider had to admit to himself that he had not handled the whole thing very well. He had been in a hurry to take a holiday. Only he knew now that men like him never got holidays. They got time off between jobs, but the next assignment was always lurking in the wings. That was what a man needed, work with a purpose to it.

He had messed it all up, but he told himself that if he got out of the mess he was in, he would never take chances again, not with his job anyway.

"One week today, Pinkerton," called William Bonney from his cell. "How's it feel? Huh?"

Raider just sat there, looking out the barred window. Where the hell was Wagner? Did it really take a week to get to El Paso from Chicago? What if it took two weeks? At least they couldn't try him and hang him in Texas. They could only take him back to Arizona to stand trial.

"You really steal them horses?" asked Billy the Kid.

Raider exhaled. "No."

Billy gave a loud guffaw. "Don't that beat all? Both of us in stir for something we didn't do. Haw, haw."

Raider had told the Kid over and over how the evidence stacked up on his behalf. He kept reassuring Billy that Wagner would come and vindicate them both. Billy said they'd probably be hung together. The Kid figured he had it coming.

"I killed my share," he had said in a dreamy voice. Then he had laughed like a boy remembering a fond afternoon from his childhood. "First was named Cahill. Frank P. Cahill. Big bully type. I was up at Messilla, just workin' with some other boys. Well, I watched old Frank as he bullied everyone. Finally got around to me. We mixed it up and he was gettin' the best of me. Then I pulled on him and shot him down. Pow. I knew right then I'd never take any guff off another livin' soul. Look at me now. Runnin' from trouble straight into it. I can't even take a few days to have some laughs without gettin' in hot water."

Raider replied, "I know what you mean."

Listening to Bonney had made him less ardent about finding the real killer of the man called Pruitt. Billy was just like all the other quick-handed punks Raider had seen in the west. He'd die before he got old, either by a bullet or a hangman's noose. Still, he had taken on the case and he hoped to finish it.

Raider grilled him, asking the Kid if he had known Norris Hand or if the sheriff had some reason to frame him. When the Kid showed an interest, Raider told him how Pruitt had been married to Hand's sister. Billy had whistled at that one, saying that they were both probably dead. Raider had then told him about the letter sent to the agency as a safeguard.

"Well at least you won't be hanged," Billy had said.

And they waited.

Ten days and Wagner still hadn't shown. Every day the same routine. Bread and water for breakfast. Wait all day. Even Bagget wouldn't come near them. He was afraid for his job. Had he forgotten about the evidence that he and Raider had come up with?

At five, the Mexican girl would bring their food. Raider had to admit that the chow in the El Paso jail wasn't bad. He wished for a cup of coffee but never got it, even after he asked.

Waiting.

No visitors, not even Tillie. Hand was afraid she would try something. He wasn't taking any chances.

At the end of the second week, Billy the Kid asked the big man: "Hey, Pinkerton, you been diddlin' Tillie?"

"Shut up, Kid."

Billy laughed. "Hey, it don't matter to me. Makes us cunt brothers, don't it? Haw, haw."

Raider felt sort of bad for Tillie. "She loves you, Kid. Don't you love her?"

Billy had a good guffaw. "Ain't that the way," he said finally. "If you don't love a woman, she's crazy about you. If you do, she don't give you the time of day."

"Tillie's gone to a lot o' trouble t' get you outta here."

"I ain't out, now, am I? Huh? That shows you what the love of a good woman does for you. Not a goddamn thing."

Raider shook his head disgustedly. "You're a shallow individual, Kid."

A laugh from William Bonney. "Yeah, if I was a creek, you wouldn't have enough water to wet your feet."

Youth, Raider thought. It brought with it a certain inability to take life seriously. Raider figured he had been acting like a kid himself. Look where he was sitting.

That evening, after the Mexican girl delivered their food, Dub Bagget slipped into the cell room to watch them eat.

"Git out of here," Billy said. "You're makin' me sick."

"I came to see the Pinkerton," Bagget replied.

He slid next to the cell door where Raider sat eating.

Raider glared at him. "Come t' gloat, deputy? Or did you come t' tell me you forgot 'bout all that evidence we found? You know, the stuff that proves ol' Henry there didn't kill Pruitt."

Bagget kept glancing over his shoulder. Then he bent close to the bars to whisper to Raider. "I ain't forgot, Pinkerton. I just can't do nothin' about it right now. When is that boss of yours gettin' here anyway?"

"Not soon enough for me," the big man replied. "You ain't heard no more word from him?"

Bagget shook his head. "Listen, don't fret none. If somethin' don't happen soon, I'm goin' up to Austin to see the marshal."

"Good," Raider replied. "Now you're thinkin'."

Bagget glanced nervously over his shoulder and then turned back. "Just one thing. Somethin' may happen. And it may happen soon. But don't bite, you got me, Pink-man? Don't take the bait or you'll be a dead catfish."

"What the hell you talkin' 'bout?"

"Dub!"

The voice had come from the office.

"That's Norris," Bagget said. "I gotta go. You remember what I said."

Raider tried to get him to stay but the deputy had to answer to his boss.

"What was that all about?" asked William Bonney.

"Nothin'," the big man replied. "Not yet, anyway."

Something was going to happen. But when? More waiting. At least until the next afternoon at five o'clock.

William Wagner was in a dither. He had spent two frustrating weeks trying to get to El Paso. Everything possible had gone wrong. Bad train connections, inclement weather, broken down steam engines, and now, just when he was less than a day away from the Texas border town, a broken wheel on the stagecoach. Traveling in the wilds of the west was enough to drive a man crazy.

"How much longer?" he asked the driver and the shotgun rider.

They were working on the wheel and didn't need a bunch of guff from some fancy-dressed dandy, even if he was some big shot with the Pinkerton agency. "Keep your shirt on," the driver said. "It ain't that bad."

The shotgun rider grinned. "Yeah, fancy-pants, don't get your balls in a uproar. We'll git you to El Paso. Guaranteed!"

Wagner exhaled and apologized to them for being so antsy. He wanted to get to Raider as soon as possible, to straighten out the case of the horses in Tucson. Pinkerton had steamed about Wagner going in person, but it had to be done. Raider's name had to be cleared for two reasons. Primarily to save the reputation of the agency; they couldn't have it said that one of their men was a horse thief. And the secondary concern was to free the big man so he could get back to work. Wagner had argued that they still needed the Arkansas roughrider to handle the more difficult cases that came through the office.

But it seemed to Wagner that he would never get to El Paso.

"Excuse me, sir."

Wagner turned to regard the well-dressed gentleman who was his fellow passenger on the stagecoach to El Paso. The gentleman in the black suit was offering him a nip from a whiskey flask. "To steady the nerves," he said, smiling.

Wagner hesitated, but then took the flask. "Thank you, Mr. Ellrod. Ordinarily I don't drink, but this trip has been something of a trial."

Ellrod chuckled sympathetically, He had a reassuring manner about him. Round, sagging face brown from the sun, rugged hands, probably a few years younger than he looked. Wagner would have taken him for a laborer of some sort, had he not been quite so eloquent in his speech.

"The west has a lot of catching up to do with the east," Ellrod said. "But a man gets used to the inconvenience of traversing long spaces. Where are you coming from, Mr. Wagner?"

"Chicago."

Ellrod nodded, flashing pale gray eyes toward the men who repaired the wheel. "Not that far east, Chicago. But I hear it's a wonderful city. You've come a long way to do your business. Let me see if I can light a fire under those two, so we can be on our way."

Wagner expressed his appreciation and then took another nip from the bottle. It was hot in Texas. He would have to exchange his narrow-brimmed bowler derby for a Stetson of some sort. Although he didn't plan to be in El Paso any longer than it took to get Raider out of town. What if the big man from Arkansas had not allowed himself to be taken into custody? What if he had shot up the whole town and killed a bunch of people?

Ellrod had moved behind the driver and the shotgun rider. "You boys need some help there?"

The driver looked back at him. "Naw, we got it just about licked, Judge. Won't be long now."

Ellrod thanked him and turned back to Wagner. "They're

doin' all right," he said. "They just want to do it correctly this time, so we don't break down again."

Wagner nodded. "I'm all for that."

Ellrod looked up at the sky. "At least there's no rain."

"Did I hear the driver call you *judge*?" Wagner asked.

Ellrod smiled. "I suppose you did. My reputation is somewhat wide in this part of Texas. I'm the circuit judge for this part of the territory. Have been for the last three years."

Wagner offered his hand. "A pleasure to meet you, Judge. I might need your legal advice and assistance when we get to El Paso."

"Oh yes? Why would that be?"

Wagner grimaced. "Well, one of my agents is in some trouble in Arizona. I have to get him out of it. I asked that the authorities in El Paso take him into custody until I get there. More to keep him out of mischief than anything else. He can be a bit of a hell-raiser, but he's really a good man."

Ellrod flashed those gray eyes. "What kind of business would you be in where you would have agents.? You with the Indian bureau?"

"Forgive me," Wagner replied. "No, I'm not with the Indian bureau. I'm with the Pinkerton Agency. Second-in-command, so to speak."

Ellrod smiled. "Well, I'd be happy to assist you. I can't offer any legal advice concerning Arizona, but I can see to it that you and your man are on your way. I know the sheriff in El Paso. He can be somewhat difficult, but he usually defers to my authority in matters like these."

Wagner deflated somewhat, wondering what else Raider might have done to get himself in trouble. Still, meeting the judge was certainly to be considered a fortunate stroke of luck. At least he would have some sway with the local authorities, even if Raider had done something to break the law.

"All set, Judge," the driver said. "You too, fancy-pants."

Wagner ignored the disrespect and got back in the coach, sitting opposite Judge Ellrod.

"Don't mind them," Ellrod said. "They like to make fun of strangers. It's the way of such men in Texas."

Wagner nodded, leaning back and closing his eyes. He fell fast asleep and began to have the strangest dream. Men were surrounding the coach, making it stop. There were five of them, all masked with guns.

Wagner opened his eyes to the reality. "My God!"

Judge Ellrod was gazing out the window. "Steady. They'll just take the strongbox. And any valuables we have. Don't get out until they tell us to."

"You're remarkably calm," Wagner offered.

Ellrod sighed. "I know this bunch. The marshals and rangers have been looking for them for months."

"All right. You in there. Come on out."

"Our cue," Ellrod said, grasping the handle of the coach door.

But he never got outside. A rifle exploded somewhere. Wagner heard a horse fall. Then the men who were robbing the coach started to fire back at someone.

Ellrod dropped to the floor of the coach. "Get down! Now!"

Wagner joined him, his hands over his head. "What the devil is going on? Who's shooting at . . . yawhh . . ."

Rifle slugs tore through the coach. Horses pounded the ground outside. Wagner could make out voices in the confusion, but he could not understand what they were shouting.

Then the shooting was over.

Ellrod got up first, looking out the coach window. "We're safe," he said.

Wagner also climbed up to the window. "Who the devil?"

Lying on the ground were the five men who had attempted to rob the coach. The shotgun rider had also been shot and he lay next to them, clutching his thigh. The five robbers had not been so lucky; they were all shot in the head and chest.

Wagner looked up and saw a group of men, riding at a lope toward the coach. "Rangers?"

Ellrod shrugged. "Maybe. Or maybe another gang planning to rob us."

"Quickly then," Wagner said. "We must get the shotgun rider into the coach and be gone."

Ellrod helped him lift the wounded man into the coach.

The riders were still approaching at a slow gallop. Where had they been hiding to fire down on the robbers? Wagner glanced toward a ridge not far away. Long shots for them. They must have known their weapons.

"Perhaps we should stay and thank them," Wagner offered.

"No," Ellrod replied. "Best to ride on. We have to get this man to a doctor."

The shotgun rider agreed that he needed immediate treatment.

Wagner deferred to the judge, figuring he knew best in matters such as these. He still would have liked to thank the men who had saved him from a dastardly fate. He had no idea that he would see the same riders again, only the next time it would be under totally different circumstances.

Raider's third week in captivity began the same as the first two. Bread and water, a long day of talking to the Kid and the terrible feeling that he would never get out of stir. At least when he had been captured by his enemies, he had always been able to plot some sort of escape, to keep his mind working in that direction.

But Wagner was on the way in this instance and he could do very little but tough it out. No chance for walking out until the legalities were cleared up. Even if Wagner didn't show, Raider would have to hire some weasel-faced lawyer to help him out. After all, they couldn't hold him forever for something he had done in another territory.

"What you thinkin' about, Pink-man?" asked Billy the Kid.

"Same old shit, Kid. Just how t' get us out o' here."

Billy laughed. "Sheeit. That'll be the day. Might as well face it, Pink. I'm gonna hang in El Paso and you're gonna hang in Arizona."

"You're dreamin', Kid."

Silence for a while from the Kid's cell. Then: "You know somethin', Pink? I do have me this dream. It's dark and I'm just standin' there. Then somebody fires out of the dark at me. I never even see who it is. I just hang there, shot to hell."

"It's only a dream, boy."

He laughed nervously. "Maybe so. Maybe so. Hell, I reckon it has to be nothin'. After all, they're gonna hang me for killin' that Pruitt. And we both know I didn't do it."

Raider leaned back on his bunk, wishing it was night. The air was cooler at night. He could sleep then.

"Hey, Pink. I wonder what we're havin' for supper tonight?"

"Don't get me thinkin' 'bout it, Kid. It's still a couple hours away."

But the Kid went on, talking about his favorite foods. Raider wondered if he was just doing it to torture him, or if he really had an appreciation of a fine meal. By five o'clock, Raider was ready to tear out the bars and go in search of a thick steak.

"Damn you, Billy!"

The key rattled in the door to the office.

"Dinnertime," said William Bonney. "Hell, I ain't even hungry now."

Raider got off his bunk. "You're a mean-minded sidewinder, Kid."

The door opened and the girl came through with the trays. She wore a hood today, surprising for the warm weather, although Raider figured a Mexican girl would be used to it. Maybe it wasn't so hot for her.

"Hey, Lupe, what'd you bring us?"

She came close to the cell with the trays. The office door closed. A pair of green eyes looked up at him.

Raider gaped into a pretty face. "Tillie!"

Bonney slammed against the bars of his cage. "Is she really here?"

Tillie started to go to Billy's cell. Raider grabbed her shoulder. "What the hell are you doin' here?"

"I bribed the Mexican girl," Tillie said. "She came to me and said she would change places with me so I could see Billy."

Raider glared at her. "Give me the trays."

"No."

"Both of them."

The Kid was reaching through the bars. "Tillie, get over here."

"Billy!"

She tried to pull away.

Raider wouldn't let go. "Give me both those trays, Tillie."

Reluctantly, she slid Raider the trays under the cell door. He let go of her and she ran to see her beau. They tried to embrace through the bars.

"Oh, Billy, I missed you so much."

The Kid's voice trembled. "I missed you too, punkin. Did you bring us anything besides food?"

Raider lifted the cloth from both trays. "She brought us plenty."

Lying on the trays, next to their supper dishes, were two firearms. Raider lifted the .38 derringer from his tray. She had brought Billy a Wells Fargo Colt pocket revolver.

"Give me one of those irons!" Bonney insisted.

Raider remembered what the deputy had said: "Don't bite, kid. It's a trick."

This was it. The trap. Bonney had his arms outside the bars. There were two cells between them, but Raider could have easily tossed one of the weapons to the Kid.

"I can't do it, Billy," the big man replied. "We been set up. It's a snare and we're the rabbits."

Tillie stepped back in front of Raider's cell. "Give me one of them guns, Raider. I mean it."

"Don't you see, Tillie?" he insisted. "That girl came to you. You didn't even know 'bout 'er. If we try t' shoot our way outta here, Sheriff Hand will blast our asses off."

"I'll take my chances with a gun," the Kid replied. "Give it up, Pink, if you really want to help me."

"I am helpin' you, Kid. That's why I gotta do this. Forgive me, Tillie, but it's the only way."

He grabbed her and socked her through the bars, knocking her unconscious.

When she slumped to the floor, he threw the guns beside her and started to cry out. "Sheriff! Sheriff get in here!"

Norris Hand came through the door with his shotgun drawn. "What the hell?"

"Tried to sneak guns to us," Raider said. "But I wouldn't have it."

Hand glared at the big man. "I oughta shoot both of you!"

For a moment, Raider thought Hand would use both barrels of the scattergun on them. But he never got the chance. William Wagner strutted into the cell room with a well-dressed man dogging his steps. He introduced himself to the sheriff and said they were there to spring Raider from his cell.

"We'll talk in my office," Hand replied. "After I send this girl on her way." He glared at Raider. "Smart move, big man.

A real smart move. You saved your life, as well as McCarty's."

Raider smiled at them. "Good to see you, Wagner."

His supervisor pointed an accusatory finger at him. "We'll see how glad you are to see me when I'm through with you."

Wagner and the well-dressed man helped Norris Hand tote Tillie's body out of the cell room.

When the door closed, Raider called to William Bonney. "Won't be long now, Kid. We'll both be outta here."

A cold voice came with the reply. "If we *do* get out of here, Pink-man, I'm gonna shoot you for hittin' my girl. Then I'm gonna shoot you for makin' me stay in this rat hole."

Strong words, the big man thought. He wondered if the Kid would ever back them up. It didn't matter now that Wagner had arrived. Things would be different as soon as he picked up the case again.

TWELVE

Wagner didn't have to talk very long to spring Raider. As Norris Hand unlocked the cell door, the big man had a funny feeling that the well-dressed man with Wagner had helped to facilitate his release. Wagner glared daggers at his most rambunctious agent, prompting Raider to feign a hangdog look.

Hand shot a dirty look at Wagner. "Get your goon out of town before I have to shoot him."

Wagner harumphed and straightened himself. "I assure you, Sheriff. You will not be bothered again by either one of us. We're going to be on the first stagecoach out of here."

"That'd bc in thc morning," Hand replied. "First thing after the roosters crow. See that you're on it."

The stranger frowned at Hand. "Sheriff, there's no need to be rude. These gentlemen are affiliated with one of the most distinguished detective agencies in the country. You'd go a long way toward using some of their methods."

Raider wasn't sure, but he thought he was beginning to like the stranger. "Much obliged, sir. What d' they call you?"

"This here's Judge Ellrod," the sheriff chimed in. "He's come to hear cases. He'll be the one to try McCarty there."

"Oh woe is me," came the howl from the Kid's cell.

Raider figured it best not to say anything in front of the judge, since he planned to present evidence in favor of the Kid.

Hand ushered them toward the front door. "Y'all would do better to take your talk out of my jailhouse."

Raider was the first one through the front door. He filled his lungs with fresh air, looking up and down the street. It felt good to be free again, even if he did have to deal with Wagner.

"To the hotel," Wagner said. "And Judge Ellrod, I'd be

obliged if you would accompany us and render your advice in certain matters."

"I'd be happy to assist you, Mr. Wagner."

Raider frowned. "Why's he gotta come along?"

"Because you're in big trouble," his supervisor replied.

"Just let me go back in an' get my guns," Raider offered.

"No!" Wagner insisted. "You're coming with me right now. Unless, of course, you no longer feel like working for the Pinkerton agency."

That hurt. Raider felt the stirring in his gut. He had suspected that his job was on the line, but it had been something else to hear it voiced by the man who could fire him.

"Aw, hell, Wagner. You won't be so mad when y' hear what I have t' say. I ain't completely loco, y'know."

"We'll discuss it when we're settled," Wagner replied.

Raider thought his boss was being a little huffy, but he figured that had always been Wagner's way.

When they were checked in, the three of them settled into a large room with enough chairs to go around.

Raider licked his lips when he saw the judge take a nip from the flask. He thought of asking for a snort, but then figured that Wagner would have a devil of fit if he started drinking. The only thing to do at first was sit back and take it. Let the banty rooster get his ire out.

"I can't tell you how poorly you handled the case in Tucson," Wagner began. "One of the ranchers filed a complaint. He suspects you of stealing his horses and selling them for twice the amount of money you handed over to the ranchers. It didn't help any that you were down in Nogales, spreading your money around in brothels and playing the big shot. Why did you have to tell people you were a horse trader?"

Raider played the hangdog-sorry gambit. "I gotta admit that didn't look too good, Wagner. But I was spendin' my back pay in Nogales. You should know, you authorized it. And I couldn't tell them people there I was a Pinkerton. What if I came back through there some day on a case? I'd be spotted in a hurry."

Wagner sighed, softening a little. "I had figured that much by myself. But this doesn't excuse the way you treated those ranchers."

"Fat men in suits," Raider replied. "'Scuse me, Judge, but it's true."

Ellrod nodded appreciatively. "I know the kind."

Raider knew he liked the stranger now.

"The others took that deal," Raider offered. "They were happy t' get back somethin'. An' hell, I had t' put my ass on the line to gouge that money outta the federales."

He left out the part about the girl helping him with the sergeant.

The big man threw out his hands. "I mean it, Wagner, those bean-eaters woulda kilt me certain if I tried t' shoot it out with 'em."

Wagner sighed. "I'm sure they would have. But what the devil were you doing south of the border?"

He could see his boss coming slowly in his direction. "I didn't rightly know where I was, Wagner. I chased Ruben Mijares till I caught 'im. Hell, them federales buried 'im deep. The whole gang."

Judge Ellrod was shaking his head. "The whole gang?" he asked admiringly.

"Yessir. There was only five of 'em. Or was it four? Hell, I don't rightly remember. But I took 'em out. And I would've brought them horses back if the federales hadn't messed me up. As it was, I managed t' make the sergeant pay me the money he had for Mijares. I also rounded up a few head o' strays t' take back. All I could find."

Ellrod whistled his appreciation. "Mr. Wagner, you got yourself one hell of a man here. If you decide to can him, we'd be happy to hire him as a territorial marshal here in the great state of Texas."

Wagner didn't seem to like the judge coming in on Raider's side. "He'll be lucky if he doesn't hang in Arizona."

"I don't know," Ellrod said. "As far as crossing the border, that doesn't make any difference. It's no crime, unless somebody could prove Raider took stolen merchandise back and forth. Which he didn't."

"Keep talkin', Mr. Ellrod," the big man cried.

Wagner glowered at Raider. "Can't you keep your mouth shut?"

"You have a pretty fair case," Ellrod continued. "The rancher who complained has to offer evidence that Raider did indeed steal his horses. He can't just go on a hunch. And it sounds like Raider went out of his way to return their property, leastways the best he could."

"I always try t' do my best," the big man said solemnly.

Wagner eased back, nodding in favor of the judge's advice. "You're right, Mr. Ellrod. The case against Raider does sound pretty thin."

Raider folded his arms, grinning triumphantly. "I been tellin' you that all along. Nothin' I did can compare to what's goin' on here in El Paso."

The judge's eyes narrowed. "What are you talking about?"

Wagner waved him off. "No need to listen to him, Judge Ellrod. He's not going to be in El Paso long enough to start any trouble."

Raider studied the likeable judge, wondering how much he should tell him. Ellrod might have to pass sentence on the men involved in the shenanigans surrounding the death of the man called Pruitt. Maybe it wouldn't suit things to have Ellrod know so much from the beginning, it wouldn't be fair.

"Judge," the big man said, "I 'preciate what all you've said in my favor. But if you ain't offended, I'd like to speak to Mr. Wagner alone."

Ellrod smiled, rising out of his chair. "Not at all."

Wagner bristled. "There's no need to be so impertinent. Why, this damnable country is full of enough ruffians. The judge and I were nearly set upon and robbed today."

Raider frowned. "Yeah? Where?"

"Just outside El Paso," Wagner replied. "We were saved only because another gang of cutthroats set upon our assailants. The judge here had enough sense to tell the driver to run from the second gang."

"One gang killed another?" Raider asked.

"Hard country," Ellrod replied. "We were just lucky."

Wagner shuddered. "I suppose we were."

Ellrod nodded to Raider. "If I was you, big man, I'd get back to Arizona and straighten out that mess before you become a name on a wanted poster. Arizona isn't a state yet and the law there still doesn't have a foothold."

Raider tipped his hat. "Much obliged, Judge."

Ellrod winked at him. "And remember what I said. If Wagner here no longer requires your services, you come to see me. I'll give you a badge and put you to work."

"Thank you, Judge Ellrod," Wagner said, "but I doubt that will be necessary. Providing that Raider is cleared of these charges, I'll have enough work to keep him busy for a year."

Ellrod closed the door behind him.

As soon as he was gone, Raider turned to Wagner. "You gotta hear this shit, Wagner. Somethin' wild is goin' on in El Paso. See, this man Pruitt was killed. Only they're tryin' to pin it on this boy who didn't do it. I got evidence, too. See . . ."

"That's enough," Wagner said. "You needn't say another word. Any entanglements you've gotten into here are inconsequential. My main concern is getting to Tucson and clearing our name."

Raider grimaced. "Wagner, that case in Tucson is over. I got some real dirt here in El Paso. Murder. And so far it all points to Norris Hand, the sheriff. You listenin'?"

Wagner frowned. "Hand? A murderer?"

"That's what I'm tryin' t' tell you. See, the man who was killed happened to be rich and he happened to be married to Hand's sister, who gets all the money now her husband's gone."

"What?"

"And they're tryin' to frame the Kid, Henry McCarty, I mean. But McCarty couldn'ta done it. 'Cause accordin' t' the deputy, Pruitt was killed with a shotgun. Billy . . . I mean, McCarty had a Navy Colt that hadn't even been fired. But Hand's tryin' t' cover it up. And there's other things, too."

Wagner sat down, suddenly interested. "Like what?"

Raider leaned forward. "Well, for one, nobody heard no shots in the alley where they say Pruitt was killed. An' somebody else heard a wagon dump a body there right afore the Kid was found with the body."

"Are these witnesses reliable?"

Raider shrugged. "More than some, less than most. But it don't matter. It didn't take me long t' convince the deputy that McCarty didn't kill Pruitt. Even if they did find him with the body."

Wagner frowned. "That looks rather bad, doesn't it? I mean, if he was found with the body . . ."

"No, not if you know all the facts. See, somebody tipped

the sheriff about where the body would be. At least that's what Hand says."

"And what do you say?"

Raider exhaled. "I think Hand killed Pruitt as sure as you and me are sittin' here. I think he dumped the body an' then waited for Billy or somebody t' come across it so he could frame 'em."

"Who's Billy?"

"I mean Henry."

Wagner glared at the big man. "Raider, is there something you're not telling me about this case?"

Raider considered telling him that the man he wanted to help was really Billy the Kid, who was wanted for other things in New Mexico. But he didn't see the need. Best just to float along until the knowledge of the Kid's identity was truly necessary.

But he had to tell Wagner something. "Okay, there's a woman in this," he offered. "She's in love with McCarty and she happens t' be a old friend o' mine. There, you satisfied?"

Wagner snorted. "Yes. I'm satisfied that you and I will leave tomorrow on the first stage bound for Tucson."

Raider didn't want to get mad so he took a deep breath. "Forget it, Wagner."

His supervisor was taken aback. "I beg your pardon?"

"I'm not leavin' that kid t' hang for somethin' he didn't do. I don't care if you fire me, I can't allow this injustice to be done."

Wagner pointed a finger at him. "Give me one good reason I should allow you to stay here and take the case on behalf of some common woman."

"Forget Tillie," the big man replied. "You owe me!"

"I owe you! For what?"

"For Kansas City, when I saved your ass," the big man replied.

Wagner glanced away. "That's not fair."

Raider stood up. "Oh, I see. It's fair for you t' drag me back t' Tucson 'cause some fat-assed rancher didn't like the way I handled his case. But it's not fair when I ask you for a chance t' help this kid."

"Raider, I . . ."

"Well fine then," the big man ranted. "I quit. Those bastards in Arizona can kiss my ass sideways. And you can kiss it too!"

"That will be enough!"

Raider grabbed the lapels of Wagner's coat, pulling him eye to eye. "Do you remember Kansas City? Huh? When you trusted that crooked policeman over me an' Doc? You remember what happened? You made us quit an' we turned out t' be right. Well I ain't gonna let that happen here!"

Wagner trembled. "What will you do?"

Raider pushed him away. "I don't know. Go get my guns an' maybe start shootin'. Maybe call Norris out. Try t' get the truth from 'im."

"You can't do that!"

Raider sighed. "I know. I been studyin' on it."

"And what did you come up with?"

He shook his head slowly, but then said: "I thought I'd look in on the widow Pruitt. See what she has t' say."

Wagner nodded. "That would be the next logical move."

Raider glanced hopefully to his superior. "You mean you're gonna let me stay on the case?"

Wagner shook his head. "No. I mean I am going to give you forty-eight hours to prove what you've told me. If I am satisfied at that point, *we* will continue the investigation. I will be the supervisory officer. Not you. Is that clear?"

"Yeah."

"Good."

"Why the change o' heart, Wagner?"

"Three reasons . . ."

"Name 'em."

"One, you seem determined, which leads me to believe you think you're right . . ."

"I know I am."

"Two, some of the facts sound solid and it seems easier to root them out than to walk away. . ."

"Couldn't have said it better myself."

"Three, I do owe you for Kansas City."

Raider nodded respectfully. "Thanks, Wagner."

"But after this," Wagner rejoined, "our debt is squared."

Raider said he was agreeable, but he fought the urge to shake hands with his bespectacled boss.

• • •

"That's the widow's house," Raider said.

Wagner stood beside him in the evening shadows. "How do you know?"

Raider grinned at his boss. "Hell, boy, I been at this awhile. I just asked round. I hope word didn't get back t' the sheriff."

Wagner sounded doubtful about the whole thing. "Hand wasn't too happy when you picked up your weapons."

"Yeah, I reckon he wasn't at that."

Wagner frowned at the big man. "What was all that business with the girl who had passed out? I never quite understood that. Hand said something about her being the girl who delivered your meals, but not much more."

"She was part of a setup," Raider replied. "McCarty's girl. Somebody paid the Mexican girl t' go t' Tillie with a plan t' spring us. Tillie brought guns with our dinner. We was supposed t' bolt, an' get ourselves shot while escapin'. Leastways that's the way I read it."

Wagner didn't say it, but he was secretly glad that Raider had fetched his guns from the sheriff's office. Hand thought they were leaving in the morning. It wouldn't hurt to poke around some, just to satisfy Raider. Maybe the big man was on to something. Maybe not. Wagner was just glad they had some protection in the Peacemaker on his agent's hip.

"Okay," Raider said. "Let's go."

They started for the front door of the widow Pruitt's house.

"Look at the size of the place," Wagner offered.

Raider chortled. "A real hacienda. Norris Hand stood t' gain a lot if Pruitt died. His sister's a wealthy woman."

"What do you know about this Pruitt?"

"He was a real town father sort," Raider replied. "Pillar o' the community, leastways that's what I heard."

As they were starting up the front steps, they heard a clicking sound. Wagner didn't know what it was, but Raider recognized it immediately. The sound of two hammers going back on a shotgun.

"Not one more step," said Sheriff Norris Hand.

He came out of the shadows with the scattergun on them.

Wagner cleared his throat. "This is not what it appears, Sheriff."

"I don't care what it appears," Hand replied. "You two are trespassin' on my property."

"Thought it was your sister's property," Raider challenged.

Hand waved the barrel of the shotgun. "Come on, both of you. I'm gonna take you back to jail and hold you there till the stage leaves in the mornin'. You'll both be on that stage. You savvy?"

Raider considered drawing down on the scattergun. But that might get both of them killed. Wagner wasn't packing and he wasn't used to gunfire. It might destroy the old boy.

"We just came t' talk t' your sister," Raider said. "'Less you're 'fraid she's got somethin' t' hide."

The front door swung open. "I have nothing to hide, gentlemen."

A grey-haired woman stuck her head out. "Norris, leave these two men alone. I'll speak to them."

Hand lowered the shotgun. "But Thelma . . ."

Thelma Hand Pruitt glared at her brother. "I said enough, young man. Now take your popgun and get back to your office."

"Aw, Thelma . . ."

But he knew he had to go.

Raider frowned a little at the way the sheriff backed down from his sister. What kind of hardened killer was controlled by an old woman? She opened the door wider and smiled, asking them in. She was still wearing black widow's weeds.

Wagner bowed to her. "We're dreadfully sorry about the intrusion, Mrs. Pruitt. But my colleague here has some rather dubious theories concerning your late husband's death."

"Then by all means come into my parlor. I'll have tea for you in a few minutes. I would enjoy some company."

Raider felt funny as he went into the fancy, lamp-lit house. He was expecting a trap, but he actually ended up with a lot less. Still, he had to keep moving, even if it didn't feel right anymore.

Wagner had just finished explaining Raider's theory to the tea-sipping Mrs. Pruitt. "So you see, Madam, you must admit that some of the evidence points directly to your brother's involvement."

She smiled, shaking her head. "No, you're totally wrong,

sir. Although I must commend your partner here."

Raider grimaced. "We ain't pardners."

Thelma Pruitt's wrinkled face slacked into a frown. "Nevertheless, young man, you have come up with something I suspected all along. There was a conspiracy to murder my husband. But my brother was not involved."

Wagner looked baffled. "Explain yourself, Madam."

She seemed sad all of a sudden, like she was remembering something painful. "My Jack was an extraordinary man. I met him in Austin. He used to be a ranger, you know. Spent many of his younger years bringing men to justice. Back then they hung them high. No trial, no tears, just a rope."

"I prefer it that way myself," Raider replied.

Wagner glared at him. "The lady is talking."

Mrs. Pruitt smiled weakly. "Don't worry, Mr. Wagner. I rather enjoy this young man's candor. He reminds me a bit of Jack."

Raider leaned forward in his chair. "Ma'am, what makes you think there was a conspiracy t' murder your husband?"

She took a deep breath, mustering her strength. "As I said before, Jack was a ranger. He liked to ride, to travel. Only lately, he had been leaving in the morning and coming back in the afternoon. Before, he'd be gone a couple of days, either hunting or fishing. But lately the trips only lasted one day. Then at night, he would come home and spend the rest of the evening in his study, poring over some papers."

"What kinda papers?" Raider asked.

"I'm not sure," she replied. "I've gone over them night after night and I can't find anything significant."

Raider stood up. "Would you mind if we had a look-see?"

"By all means," she replied. "But you must promise me one thing."

"What's that?"

"You must rule out my brother as a suspect."

The big man nodded, but said, "The truth will lead us, Ma'am. If we uncover somethin' awful, ever'body has t' live with it."

Thelma Pruitt stood up. "My husband's study is down that hall. You will be kind enough to let yourselves out when you're finished."

Wagner bowed a little. "My humble apologies for our disturbance, Madam."

She smiled politely. "On the contrary. It has been delightful. Good night, gentlemen. May the good Lord guide you in your quest."

"Raider, look at this."

They had almost given up, working their way to the bottom of Jack Pruitt's papers. Now Wagner had a couple of strange looking parchments in his hand.

"What is it?" the big man asked.

Wagner held up the three pieces of paper. Squiggly lines were drawn in seemingly random geometrical shapes. There was a huge red dot at the center of the black lines. Smaller red dots were scattered throughout.

"Some kind of map?" Wagner asked.

Raider nodded. "Maybe. All three drawings look the same."

Wagner glanced over his shoulder. "There's a map of the county on the wall there. Let's see . . ."

For a while they tried to line everything up, but it didn't work. Wagner took a closer look at the map on the wall. He must have studied it for ten minutes before he cried out.

"There. A small red dot." He looked at the other papers. "It seems to be the same red ink."

Raider squinted at the map. "Place called Red Clay Flats. Just north o' town. That's good, Wagner. You ever think 'bout becomin' a detective?"

His boss did not appreciate the joke. "Don't forget who's in charge of this investigation now."

"I ain't forgot," Raider replied sheepishly. "In fact, I was just about t' ask you what you'd do next."

Wagner sighed. "Well, Mrs. Pruitt seems awfully convinced that her brother is innocent."

"Yeah and I can't believe she's workin' with 'im either, not after the way she let us in here t' have a look-see."

Wagner nodded. "Nothing here, except these maps. And that dot on the wall map. The two could be related, but what's the significance?"

The big man decided to play Devil's advocate. "Could be just a land deal or somethin'."

"Maybe," Wagner said, obviously enraptured by the case. "But Jack Pruitt was working on something before he was killed. And he was working on it alone."

Raider gestured back to the wall. "I vote for Red Clay Flats."

"For what?"

He shrugged. "Let's ride out there an' poke around. Take these papers with us. See if anythin' matches up."

"But I don't have a horse."

"We'll take Tillie's buggy," the big man replied. "Or if you're up to it, you can ride her harness-bred."

"And what if I don't want to go to Red Clay Flats?" Wagner challenged.

Raider grinned. "Then I go without you."

"I'm in charge here!"

"So what'll it be, pardner?"

Wagner sneered at the word "partner," but then he softened some and said, "We're going out to Red Clay Flats. Is that agreeable to you?"

Raider said that it was.

THIRTEEN

Wagner sat in the saddle of a gentle roan mare rented from the livery in El Paso. Raider rode his grey, which seemed to be tireless no matter how far he pushed it. Of course, on the ride to Red Clay Flats, the big man had to take it easy. Wagner couldn't maintain a steady pace—unless you counted the way he ran his mouth.

"Murder most foul," said the bespectacled supervisor. "I've often wondered what pushed a man to commit murder. Is it simple emotion or something that lies in the opportunistic nature of the creature? How does one work up enough courage to pull the trigger, to stick the knife into a man's back?"

Raider shifted in the saddle. "It's easy to stick somebody who won't shut up," he muttered under his breath.

"I beg your pardon?" Wagner asked.

"Nothin'."

Their horses plodded on. It couldn't be much further to Red Clay Flats, or at least that was what Raider hoped. Listening to Wagner reminded the big man of his former partner, Doc Weatherbee, who had also been longwinded. He realized how much he had come to enjoy working alone. It was a lot quieter.

But his boss had no intention of shutting up. "Now take that McCarty, for instance. Let's say he did shoot Pruitt."

"But he didn't."

Wagner shot a stern look at the big man. "But for argument's sake, let's say he did."

"Unh."

"Now what would make him pull the trigger? Was he hired? Did he have a personal grudge against Pruitt?"

Raider sighed. "Maybe Pruitt wouldn't stop yappin'."

"What?"

"Nothin'."

Wagner shook his head. "I still don't understand what drives a man to kill another man."

Raider shrugged. "Sometimes it's as simple as a disagreement. Tempers fire up an' guns get drawed. Shootin', knifin'. It don't make any difference. Seems to me like that's one thing men do best; killin' each other."

Wagner harumphed. "That's a rather cynical attitude, Raider."

He wasn't sure what "cynical" meant, but he replied: "Wagner, I seen men killed an' I killed 'em ever' way possible. An' the only thing I can tell you is this. You take the worst savage Injun off the reservation an' put 'im next t' one o' them downtown bankers you deal with in Chicago. Then you put pressure on both of 'em. Threaten their lives an' see what happens. You know what you'll find?"

Wagner was gazing out over the rolling plain, a bit peeved that Raider had taken charge of their dialogue. "What?"

"You're gonna find that there ain't much diff'rence between the man in a suit and the man in buckskins. You'll find that men kill sometimes because they have to, sometimes because they want to, an' sometimes because they just plain damn *like* it."

"I heartily disagree," Wagner replied. "I've never felt the urge to kill anyone!"

Raider grinned at him. "Not even me?"

That shut him up.

They kept riding over the uneven terrain. Raider would look at the map once in a while and then gaze up at the sky to try to figure out how long they had been riding. According to the map, Red Clay Flats couldn't have been more than a half day's ride. They had left El Paso around seven in the morning and it was almost noon.

"Oughta be there soon," he said to Wagner.

No reply from the petulant man on the mare.

They pushed on into a stiff wind that started up hot and sandy from the north. Raider put a bandanna over his face. Wagner endured the flying grit until the big man offered him a bandanna from his saddlebags.

Clouds were rolling down behind the wind. Rain maybe. Raider only had one slicker with him. Wagner would just have to get wet if it started to fall. At least the loquacious gentleman had been possessed of enough good sense to buy a wide-brimmed Stetson to keep the sun off his face.

When they came over a knotty rise, Raider made a pronouncement. "Red Clay Flats," he said blankly.

Wagner raised an eyebrow. "Are you sure?"

"Look at the ground. Ol' Texas red clay. Not good for much 'cept buryin' dead cowboys."

Wagner didn't find the joke very funny. "What the devil could Pruitt have discovered in a place like this?"

Raider nudged the grey, starting to swing in a wide circle. "I don't know, Wagner. If I had knowed, we wouldn'ta come out here, would we?"

"Raider, I don't appreciate your tone one bit. If you wish to stay on in the employ of the Pinkerton agency. . ."

"That's another thing," Raider said. "I'm gettin' kinda tired o' you holdin' my job over me. It's bad 'nough that you bull in here an' start tellin' me how t' run things, but I don't care if I stay on or not, not if it means listenin' t' your bull-shit."

Wagner didn't quite know what to say to that.

Raider gestured to his right. "You ride in that direction, Boss. I'll go this way. We'll meet at them hills yonder."

He pointed to the gradual rise about a half mile away.

Wagner gawked. "What are we looking for?"

"Anythin'," the big man replied. "Only it won't be ordinary. Not if Jack Pruitt was spendin' so much time out here."

"If you say so."

"Wagner?"

"Yes."

"You got a gun?"

Wagner shook his head. Raider reached into his vest pocket and took out his .38 derringer. He tossed it to Wagner, who barely managed to catch it.

"You know how t' use it?"

Wagner exhaled disgustedly. "No. And I doubt if I'll have to."

Raider shrugged. "You never know. Just try t' stay where I can see you. This place ain't big, so it shouldn't take too long t' cover it."

"If you say so."

They started away in different directions, both of them scanning the ground for any signs of a clue.

Raider had to laugh a little at the way Wagner had reacted to the gun. The big man offered him the derringer just to get his goat. He knew Wagner didn't know much about firearms. And the derringer wouldn't give him much of a chance against a bigger weapon, but it was better than nothing.

The grey clomped over the reddish earth of the clay flat, making for the hills in the distance. Nothing but dirt, Raider thought. Several hundred acres of ground that wouldn't even grow cotton. Homesteaders wouldn't take the land if you gave it to them with a couple of mules.

So why had Jack Pruitt been so fascinated with this stretch of red plain? Was he going to buy it? For what?

Word had it that the railroad was coming, but Raider knew from experience that land for those kinds of deals was bought up well in advance. Besides, the tracks were coming down from the northeast, not due north, where Red Clay Flats was situated in relation to El Paso.

Still, Jack Pruitt had been a smart man. He wouldn't have bought up a bad stretch of ground unless he had a good reason—if he intended to buy it in the first place. Maybe they could ask a few questions in town. Check with the town clerk about deeds and such. Find out who owned the land.

The grey snorted and began to dance nervously. Raider looked down, wondering what had spooked the animal. He glanced across the plain to see Wagner's mare moving slowly along. There was nobody else in the area, as far as he could see.

He patted the animal's neck. "What is it boy?"

Raider sniffed the air. Maybe the grey smelled something. He rode a few more feet before he smelled something too. He turned his face to the wind. Nothing there. The musty odor seemed to be coming from the ground itself. What did that damned odor remind him of?

"Raider!"

The big man looked over his shoulder. Wagner was coming straight at him, riding as fast as he could without falling out of the saddle. What the hell had him so riled up?

"Riders," Wagner said. "Four or five of them."

Raider peered toward the horizon. "Which way?"

"From the east," Wagner replied. "It was strange. I heard them before I saw them. Then I could make out their dust."

Thunder cracked overhead. A rainstorm was coming. They'd have to take shelter anyway.

"Let's make for them hills," Raider said.

Wagner looked back to the east. "But what about those riders?"

"We'll keep an eye on 'em. They're probably just passin' through. Come on, before we get wet."

They turned their mounts and drove hard for the hills to the north.

The rain never came down, at least not on Red Clay Flats. The storm moved quickly to the south, heading straight for El Paso. It was a good thing too, Raider thought, because the hills didn't have any cover to use as a hiding place from the rain. However, the rise did have a good vantage point that allowed them to look straight down on the flats.

"There they are," Wagner said, pointing toward the riders.

Raider grunted. "They'll probably just keep goin'."

He couldn't have been more wrong, to the obvious delight of Wagner.

As the bespectacled gentleman had said, there were five horses. However, only four of the horses held riders. The fifth mount carried a man slung over the saddle with his belly down—the way you loaded a dead man.

"One of them boys had some back luck," Raider offered.

Wagner squinted at the horsemen. "Strange."

"What?"

He shook his head. "Nothing."

"Go on, say it," the big man urged.

"Well, it's just that . . . I don't know, it sounds silly but I seem to recall having seen those men before."

Raider grimaced. "You sure?"

"Yes!" Wagner replied. "When we were being robbed on the stagecoach. They look like the four men who shot the bandits that were robbing us."

Raider rolled his eyes. "Right. You rec'nize 'em now after you ran away before. How far were they from you?"

"About this same distance."

Raider exhaled. "All riders look alike from that far away."

"Look," Wagner said, pointing toward the horsemen. "They're stopping."

Raider glanced back toward the flats. "Son of a gun. They are. Hell, Wagner, maybe we got somethin' here."

The riders dismounted and went to work quickly. Two of them pulled small shovels from their saddlebags and began to dig. The other two unlashed the dead man and rolled him onto the ground.

"Looks like they're gonna bury 'im," Raider said.

Wagner frowned. "This isn't a cemetery."

Raider snapped his fingers. "That's it. That's what I smelled out there. It was just like a Injun burial ground."

Wagner was transfixed. "Who could they be burying?"

"We'll have t' wait an' see."

Wagner wasn't sure what the big man meant by that and he was afraid to ask. They just kept watching as the two riders dug a shallow grave in the red earth. When the grave was finished, the other two men dragged the body over and laid it to rest in the hole. They all took turns covering it up.

"No cairn, no headstone," Raider said. "A tough way t' go. No preacher t' say some good words."

Wagner shuddered. "What does this have to do with anything that's going on in El Paso?"

"Can't say," the big man replied. "Shit!"

"What?"

The men were climbing back onto their horses.

"I wish I could see their faces. At least I can remember their mounts. Two blacks, a sorrel, an' a pinto. That dead boy was on a mule."

Wagner nodded. "Good thinking, Raider."

"We'll see. Shit, one of 'em picked up our tracks." Raider drew his Colt. "I sure as hell hope they don't come this way."

Wagner had suddenly turned ghost-white. "Neither do I."

"We might be able t' talk to 'em like we didn't see a thing," Raider offered. "Tell 'em we're out here lookin' for a place t' go huntin'. Course, that would give us a chance t' see their faces. Then again . . ."

"What?" Wagner asked nervously.

"Remember what you was sayin' 'bout killin'?"

The pale man nodded.

"Well, old buddy, you might just get a chance t' find out, firsthand."

The riders argued among themselves for a while. One of them pointed out the tracks, arguing that the four of them should go in that direction. Probably want to see if anyone spotted them, Raider thought. But one of them, the man who seemed to be in charge, finally convinced the others to ride back toward the east, where they had come from.

Raider breathed easier. "Well, that's a load off my mind. It's a good thing they were in a hurry."

"Yes, it was."

He decided to play with Wagner a little. "Yep, my old trusty Colt mighta got three of 'em, but you woulda had t' take the fourth one with your derringer."

"What makes you think they would have tried to kill us?"

Raider nodded toward the fresh grave. "They killed that one, didn't they?"

"Well, yes."

"Okay, let's go dig 'im up an' see who he is."

"Raider!"

The big man glanced at his superior. "You got any better ideas?"

Wagner gaped at him. "Well, I . . . I mean, robbing a grave."

"That ain't it at all," Raider replied. "This ain't exac'ly what you call holy ground. There wasn't no preacher, so it ain't really right with God yet. Is it?"

"I suppose not. But we should notify someone. Go back to El Paso and tell the authorities."

"Who? Norris Hand? One of our prime suspects, even if his sister says he's innocent?"

Wagner still didn't like the idea. "We could tell the judge."

Raider shook his head. "We'd waste a whole day gettin' back there an' then ridin' back out here. Nope, the best way t' do it is t' dig up that boy an' see if there's a clue to his name buried with 'im."

"I do not see what this has to do with our case back in El Paso!"

"Maybe nothin'. Maybe ever'thin'. Hell, you were the one who found the clue that led us t' Red Clay Flats. Maybe Pruitt knew about what was goin' on out here. Maybe that's why he was killed."

No matter how hard he tried, Wagner could not find a hole in the logic of Raider's proposal. Still, he did not want to be a ghoul, even if it did clear up a few things. It just didn't seem right.

Raider started down the hill for the horses. "You can stay here if you want, William. Course, I'd hate for you t' be alone if them four came back. Seein's how you only got two shots in that derringer."

"Damn your black eyes!"

"Funny, Doc used t' say the same thing."

"When this is over . . ."

"Let's just hope we're both alive when this is over," Raider offered. "Now come on, let's get our hands dirty."

Raider had a two-fold plan. First, dig up the body and see what he could figure out from the corpse. Then follow the tracks of the four men to see if he could find them. It seemed like a good ploy until the rain circled back and began to fall on them.

Digging in the wet clay was almost impossible, even with the freshly turned earth of the grave. Each time Raider scooped up two handfuls of red dirt, the wet mess collapsed back in on itself. It took him nearly a half hour to dig out enough clay to reveal the buried man's cold blue hand.

Wagner stepped back when he saw the bloated fingers.

"Been dead a while," was all Raider said. He looked up at his boss, who was now wet and pitiful. "This would be a lot easier if you'd help."

But Wagner just didn't have it in him.

Raider went back to work by himself, digging out around the shape of the corpse. After another hour of scooping mud by hand, he was able to pull the body out of the hole. Wagner gawked at the death-blue face of the unfortunate soul who had been laid to a stormy rest on Red Clay Flats. His eyes were open and his mouth gaped in a final expression of horror.

"My God, Raider, is this really necessary?"

The big man from Arkansas just dragged the body away from the grave, leaving it in the rain.

"What are you doing?" Wagner asked.

Raider looked up at the cloudy sky. "Let the heavens wash 'im clean afore I start pokin" round on 'im. Hell, he's dressed like every drifter I ever saw. Can't say I rec'nize 'is face. Course, it's swelled up a little. You gotta admit, though, he don't stink much."

Wagner turned away, vomiting.

Raider waited a while before he went over the corpse, searching the pockets of the dead man. Wagner stood with his back to the eerie spectacle. He wasn't sure that Raider's actions coincided with proper procedure, but he had come to expect such behavior from his unruly sidekick.

"Look here, Wagner."

Raider was coming toward him with something in hand.

Wagner gawked at the wanted poster Raider had taken from the man's pockets. "What does that have to do with anything?"

Raider gestured back toward the corpse. "'Less I'm way off, that dead one is Dagwood Sweeney. Called Woody by some, Dag by others. Here, says so on the poster. And take a gander at this."

He handed Wagner a crudely made silver ring, a thin band taken from the dead man's finger.

"You know what that is?"

Wagner shook his head.

"Prison ring," Raider replied. "Men make 'em while they're servin' out their sentences. Bang down a silver dollar with a spoon, then drill out the center. I seen 'em afore."

Wagner had suddenly become interested in the bizarre detective work done by his most colorful agent. "So this Sweeney just got out of prison?"

Raider tipped back his Stetson. "Not recent-like. He ain't wearin' the clothes they give you when you leave the rock pile. No, he been out a while. But he served 'is time. That poster's an old one."

"Why would he keep it on him?"

Raider shrugged. "That kind is proud o' what they done. Probably had it on 'im since afore he was captured."

Wagner rubbed his chin. "So why was he killed and buried by those men?"

"Well, ordinarily, I'd say he was a gang member with 'em. Maybe they double-crossed 'im an' he found out. Or he double-crossed them an' they decided t' end it."

"That makes sense," Wagner said.

Raider shook his head. "Not this time."

His superior squinted at him. "Explain yourself."

"Well, two things. First, he wasn't shot. He was hanged. The marks round his neck show that. And it ain't like a outlaw t' hang one o' his own. Men that live by the gun would rather die that way. Even if Sweeney had crossed his own boys, they woulda done 'im the service o' pluggin' 'im right, even if it was in the back."

Wagner shivered. "You certainly have an understanding of the criminal mind, Raider. It's almost frightening."

"Ain't it?"

"You said there were two things."

Raider's sleight of hand produced a faded newspaper clipping that was almost crumbling in the rain. "Found this on 'im, too. It's a story 'bout a man that's been robbin' settlers; you know, farmers, sodbusters, nesters. The description of the man in the story fits Sweeney and there's even some speculation that Sweeney was the one t' do the robbin', though it's widely knowed that Sweeney operated closer t' the Oklahoma/Texas border. This clip comes from a paper north o' here, in Austin. Guess Sweeney went back into 'is old bus'ness."

"So those men buried an outlaw?"

Raider nodded. "Sweeney weren't exac'ly the salt o' the earth. Some even say he killed 'is own father."

Wagner took a deep breath. "As much as I hate to say this, Raider. Good work."

The big man grimaced. "Well, not exac'ly. I would like to go find those men that planted Sweeney, though."

"Yes, they must be brought to justice."

"Justice? Hell, I wanted t' shake their hands."

Wagner eyed him disdainfully. "No one can operate outside the law, Raider. Lynchings should be a thing of the past. Although, how do we know that those men weren't representing some law, say the Rangers or maybe one of the marshals in this area?"

"No way," the big man replied.

"How can you be so certain?"

"Easy," he replied, "the Rangers wouldn't go t' the trouble o' draggin' Sweeney all the way out here. Neither would a marshal. Hangin's a big thing an' lawmen take advantage o' the event t' scare anybody who's been thinkin' 'bout a life o' crime. Course, nobody'd be discouraged if they were dead set on robbin' an' killin'. Some men are just plain bad."

Wagner sniffed a little. "A stirring assessment of the criminal kind. Obvious, but stirring."

"Why you little . . ."

"Don't say it, Raider. Not if you value your job."

"Maybe you'd just like t' finish this case by yourself. I mean, I could take off and nobody'd ever find me, not even them lily-livered ranchers in Tucson."

They endured a moment of awkward silence that was ended by an increase in rainfall.

Wagner looked at the body. "Well, I suppose we better get our friend there back to El Paso."

"No."

"What?"

Raider exhaled, fatigued by digging. He was trying to be patient with his superior, even if it was almost impossible. Wagner bristled at the big man's negative reply.

"Why shouldn't we take him back?"

"Just this," Raider said. "Jack Pruitt had this place marked on 'is map. Somebody killed 'im. What d'you think would happen t' us if we went back t' El Paso, sayin' we found a burial ground with a bunch o' bodies planted in it? Huh? How long you think it would be afore somebody shot us in the back?"

Wagner sputtered. "I . . . but . . . wait a minute. You think other bodies are buried out here besides Sweeney?"

"My nose told me there were. And my head is willin' t' go along. And if we want t' find out what's goin' on, we'll put Sweeney back an' ride on back t' El Paso. That way nobody knows we found this place."

Wagner peered out over the flats. "More bodies. Damn it all. What have we gotten into?"

"Deep shit."

"We'll go to the marshal," Wagner offered officially. "We'll take our evidence to the Rangers too."

"That don't get it. Not if we want t' stay on a hot trail. By the time we went t' the law, who's t' say them four won't get wind that we're on to them. No way we could surprise them then."

Wagner raised an eyebrow. "Then you agree that these men must be brought to justice?"

The big man nodded reluctantly. "Yeah, I reckon. As much as I'd like t' see Sweeney's kind killed off, I gotta admit that it should be done legal-like. Though we have yet t' prove them men was operatin' outside the law."

"Chances are that they were."

"Chances are." Raider looked back at the body. "Hell, I reckon I better plant 'im. If that's all right with you."

Wagner thought about it for a while. He probably would have cogitated forever if the rain weren't pelting him. Raider would abide by Wagner's judgment; providing that Wagner decided in favor of Raider's course of action.

"All right," Wagner said finally. "Bury Sweeney. Then we'll go back to El Paso. It's certain we can't follow those four men, not with the rain to wash out their tracks. I do want to get to the bottom of this. And I have to admit that you're on top of things so far, Raider."

"You won't regret it, Boss."

"I hope not. I'd settle for getting out of this alive."

Dead men didn't have any regrets, Raider thought. None at all. Just ask Dagwood Sweeney. He didn't give a damn if red clay covered him. He didn't care if the earth swallowed him up for a second time.

FOURTEEN

Darkness was on them by the time they saw the silhouette of El Paso in the distance. A few lights twinkled to guide them toward the border town. The ride back had taken longer than usual since Wagner could not handle a full gallop on the mare. Raider still thought his boss was a pain in the ass, but he had to admit that he was gaining respect for Wagner. The four-eyed little man was hanging in and deferring to Raider's judgment on the close calls.

The big man reined up when they were near the edge of town.

Wagner also stopped, casting a curious glance in Raider's direction. "What now?" he asked.

Raider eyed him, figuring something. "You can't ride straight back t' the hotel," he said. "Too risky."

Wagner bristled. "I want to take a bath and get out of these wet clothes. I don't see the harm in . . ."

"Think of it like this:" Raider offered, "by now, ever'body in El Paso knows we didn't leave. They know you rented the mare an' that we rode outa town t'gether. Might not be wise t' do what they think we're gonna do, leastways till we see which way the wind's blowin'."

Wagner nodded, relenting to Raider's instinct. The rough-hewn Arkansas hillbilly had a second sense about such things. Wagner was beginning to respect the need for anticipation in field work. Perhaps he had been behind a desk for too many years.

"All right," he said. "What do you suggest I do?"

Raider took off his slicker and handed it to Wagner. "Put this on. Then pull your hat real low. Ride round t' the west, circle in on the other side o' town. There's an alley, 'bout halfway along there. You'll see a buggy an' some stairs leadin' up to a little place that belongs to a friend o' mine. Just tell 'er you know me an' she'll let you in."

"A woman?"

"Tillie. The one what got me into all this. Don't fret, she's a good girl, my kind o' woman."

Wagner frowned. "That's what I'm afraid of." But he still put the slicker on and pulled his hat low.

"You look like a real desperado, William. Only a little smaller."

Wagner blushed, but held his tongue. "Tillie?"

"She ain't gonna bite you. Hell, you're a gent. Just treat her like a lady an' she'll be eatin' outta your hand."

"Quite!"

"And tell 'er t' put on a stewpot. I could eat dead skunk I'm so hungry."

The big man started to turn the tireless grey toward the twinkling lights.

Wagner looked at him. "Raider?"

Raider glanced over his shoulder. "What?"

"Well, I just wanted to tell you that you've done some fine detective work so far. I . . ."

"You never shut up, do you?"

"Why I never!"

"No, I guess you don't. Just wait for me till I get back."

Wagner shouted as Raider started away. "Where are you going?"

Raider called back. "To see the Kid."

Wagner watched for a moment as the big man galloped off toward the town.

Then he turned the mare west and started slowly for Tillie's place.

Raider thundered down the main street, which was deserted in the dark rain.

A light burned in the sheriff's office. The big man stabled the grey and stomped across the muddy street to the jailhouse. When he pushed open the door, Deputy Bagget dropped his feet off the desk.

"Raider! Where the hell you been? I been lookin' all over for you."

"Where's Hand?"

Bagget shrugged. "Don't know. It's my watch tonight. Listen, I been nosin' around but I ain't found out nothin'."

Raider glanced toward the cell room. "We'll hash it out later. Right now I gotta see the Kid."

"Sure. Damn, what you been doin' anyway? You're as dirty as a pig sty after a rain storm."

"Bagget, I ain't got time to pussyfoot. Let me in to see Bonn . . . McCarty. We can talk after I get a few things straight."

"Okay, okay. You're as touchy as an old cook."

Raider exhaled defeatedly. "Sorry, old buddy. I just gotta ask that boy a few questions."

Bagget frowned. "You sound different. Like you might think he's really got somethin' to hide."

"Let me in and I'll find out."

He intended to get the truth out of Billy the Kid if he had to shoot him to do it.

Wagner found the alley without too much trouble. He tied up his mount, fetching a feed bag from the saddlebags provided by the livery man. "Just feed her if you don't get back here tonight," the man had said. "She's steady but she's got to be fed."

He trudged up the stairs, his hand inside his pocket, closed around the derringer Raider had given him. After seeing the dead man, he felt more secure with a ready weapon in his grip. What if he had the wrong door?

He knocked.

No answer.

He knocked again.

"Who is it?" a soft voice said.

"I'm William Wagner . . ."

"Don't know you."

". . . a friend of Raider's."

The door opened immediately.

Wagner was taken aback by the beauty of the young lady who stood before him. She hardly seemed the type that Raider usually went for. She smiled warmly at him.

"Are you Tillie?"

She nodded. "Yeah. I reckon Raider's mad at me for that

business in the jail, when I tried to break them out. Did he tell you about it?"

Wagner looked confused. "Oh, was that you?"

"Hey, you were there!" Tillie said. "You were with another old guy."

Wagner blushed. "Yes, another old guy," he said sadly. "Excuse me, Miss, but if it's no trouble, this old man would like to get out of the rain. Raider asked me to wait here for him."

She opened the door wider. "Come right in, Sir. Goodness, I bet you're all wet under that slicker. We have to get you dried off."

Wagner was relieved at the cosy enclosure of her room. It was warm and filled with soft, orange lamplight. Tillie helped him off with the slicker and then started to unbutton his coat.

Wagner stopped her. "My dear girl . . . please, I don't think it proper if I were to . . ."

Tillie brushed wet hair from his forehead. "Now, now, William, you don't want to catch your death of cold. Why, if you was to come down with the grippe, Raider would never forgive me."

"But I . . ."

"Oh, don't fret," she replied, winking at him. "I've seen thousands of men in their skivvies."

"No, it isn't right."

Tillie put her hand on his shoulder. "I'll git you a blanket. And you can soak your feet in hot water. I'll heat it for you on the stove. We can hang your suit up to dry."

Wagner could no longer resist her. He insisted she avert her eyes while he exchanged his wet clothes for the blanket. When he was all wrapped up, Tillie shook his clothes and then hung them over the stove to dry. Wagner perched uneasily on the bed, wondering how he had let Raider get him into such a mess. He had not had such a busy day in a long time.

"Here you go, William. Hot water."

She came toward him with a steaming tub for his cold feet.

Wagner sucked air through his teeth when his feet hit the water.

Tillie took a towel and began to dry his head. "There, don't you feel a whole lot better now?"

Wagner nodded. "Thank you."

He sneezed.

Tillie patted him on the shoulder. "I'm gonna get you some hot soup."

"Thank you, kind lady."

"You talk just like a gentleman."

Wagner tried to smile. "One hopes."

When he had finished his soup, Tillie made him lie back on the bed. She rubbed his feet and legs, trying to work out some of the soreness. Wagner had to admit that it felt good. A day in the saddle had left him almost unable to move. He wondered how Raider lived on a saddle day in and day out.

Tillie brushed back the blanket, baring his midsection. "Goodness."

Wagner tried to sit up. "Young woman."

"Oh, don't be bashful, William. From the look of your whanger, you could use a good . . ."

"I insist that you . . ."

"Umm, that's not so bad. Old guys can do what young guys do. It just takes them a little longer."

She was touching him.

What would Pinkerton have thought if he knew?

Damn it, she knew what she was doing. It felt good. After a rainy ride across the plain, he felt a need to indulge himself.

"Comin' right along," Tillie said. "Oh, you are a good boy, William. I just knew you would be."

He hadn't been that way in ages.

Tillie started to lift her skirt.

Wagner closed his eyes. "Tillie, you must never tell anyone."

"Not even Raider?"

"Especially him."

She straddled him. "Okay. Ooh. You're such a good boy William."

In spite of their pleasure, Wagner was not sure he could agree with her.

Billy the Kid sat up on his bunk when Raider appeared at the door of his cell. "Pink-man. Thought I'd seen the last of you. Hey, you know my trial is Monday. You gonna be there?"

"Get up, boy."

"What?"

Raider motioned with his hand. "Come over here where we can talk."

Bonney rose and sidled up to the bars. "What the hell you been doin' anyway? You look like you . . ."

Raider reached through the bars, grabbing Bonney, pulling him against the door. "Now you listen up, Kid. I seen some shit today. There's four riders buried a body out on Red Clay Flats. They was ridin' two blacks, a sorrel, an' a pinto. The body belonged to Dagwood Sweeney. You know anythin' 'bout that?"

Bonney was wide-eyed, almost afraid of the big man's temper. "Hey, let go of me. I mean it."

Raider reached down and grabbed his Colt, thumbing the hammer, putting the bore against Bonney's temple. "Talk, Billy. Or they'll be scrapin' your brains off the wall with a trowel."

Bagget came up behind Raider. "Hey, what the hell are you . . ."

"Back off, deputy. This is between me and the Kid."

Bonney nodded, frozen with fear. "Okay, big 'un. You just put that gun back in your holster. You let go of me and I'll talk."

Bagget started back for the office. "I don't want to be part of this, Raider. You holler when you're finished."

Raider eased off, pulling the gun away from the Kid's head, letting go of him. "What do you know about those riders?"

Billy rubbed his sore chest, where he had banged against the bars. "I don't know a damned thing. Hey, Pink, give me that gun. Let me shoot my way out, or at least have a chance to try."

He pointed a finger at Bonney. "You better get straight, boy. They're gonna string you up if you don't. I'm the only chance you got. Now you tell me what you know 'bout Red Clay Flats."

Billy sighed. "Raider, I don't know a damned thing about Red Clay Flats. I'm from New Mexico, remember?"

"Nothin' 'bout those men?"

The Kid thought about it for a couple of minutes. "All right, there was this one boy up in Lincoln County, rode a pinto. Name was Murph Hizer. He rode with the Regulators same time as me. Only he didn't stay long. He headed east. Last I heard he was in San Antonio."

"That's it?"

"Hey, what else can I tell you?"

Raider eyed him closely. "An' Red Clay Flats don't mean a thing t' you?"

"Not rightly. I reckon I have heard of that Sweeney boy. But he was in prison, wasn't he?"

The big man shook his head. "Not anymore. Somebody hung 'im an' planted 'im in the ground."

Bonney rubbed his own neck, frowning. "Can't imagine Hizer would hang a man like Sweeney. They'd most likely be friends."

Raider shrugged. "Maybe. But there's some strange shit goin' on round here an' nothin' would s'prise me at this point."

"Not even me?"

Raider wheeled to see Norris Hand standing in the doorway with the twin barrels of his scattergun aimed at the big man's chest.

"You got some bad habits," Hand said. "What the hell are you doin' here?"

Raider's eyes narrowed. "I been ridin', Hand. All the way out t' Red Clay Flats!"

He studied the sheriff's reaction. Hand was cool customer. He didn't even blink. Like Red Clay Flats didn't mean a thing to him.

"That ain't no business of mine, Pinkerton. I just want you out of my jail in a hurry. We got to get ready for a trial."

"Been to any funerals lately?" Raider continued. "Or han-gin's?"

Hand grimaced. "What the hell are you talkin' about? We ain't gonna hang McCarty here till after the trial."

"You're one hell of a weasel, Norris. Smilin' just like you ain't been in the henhouse."

Hand gestured with the shotgun. "Come on, Pink. You can tell it to somebody who'll listen. Only it'll be outside this jailhouse."

Raider started slowly toward the sheriff. "You wouldn't happen t' know where the judge is, would you?"

Hand blinked at that one. "You stay away from Mr. Ellrod. Anything you say to him can be said at the trial."

"I warn you, Hand. I got a lotta evidence on the Kid's behalf. You're gonna look like a fool."

Hand grinned. "Depends on how many of my cousins they got on the jury," the sheriff replied. "Don't it?"

Raider pushed past him, looking for the deputy. "Where's Bagget?"

Hand still had that self-satisfied grimace on his face. "I sent him home. I also told him not to talk to you."

The big man pointed a finger back at him. "I know 'bout Red Clay Flats, Sheriff. If you got anythin' t' do with that, I'll tear you up."

"You picked a terrible place to know about, Pink. I never even been up there. Nothin' but dirt and gravel."

Raider gave him one more look and then turned and went out into the street.

The rain was coming softer now, a fine mist in the diffused lights of El Paso. Raider started for Tillie's through the mud. Hand hadn't bitten on the quick reference to Red Clay Flats. Maybe there wasn't a connection.

Still, it made sense that Hand was in on the demise of Jack Pruitt, who had been casing Red Clay Flats for some unknown reason—unless you counted the unorthodox burial ground. Raider wondered if he had stumbled onto something bigger that just the Pruitt killing. Hell, Pruitt had been a Ranger once. Maybe he had been in charge of the burial detail at Red Clay Flats. Although Raider was pretty sure Pruitt had been done in because he simply *knew* about the burials on the flats. How were they going to talk anyone into going out there and digging up the evidence?

Raider stopped for a moment, trying to remember which alleyway led to Tillie's place.

He heard splashing behind him.

He looked around to see the shadow coming along the street, some two blocks back.

Raider kept on, turning into the alley at the corner of the right building. As he slid around into the darkness, he leaned back against the wall, waiting to see if the shape was following him. Sure enough, a man turned into the alley within a few seconds.

Bursting out of the shadows, Raider tackled the man at the knees, knocking him into the mud. They wrestled for a few moments, until Raider came out on top. He lifted a fist to slam into the man's face.

"Raider, it's me, Bagget!"

He stopped the punch before it reached the deputy's round face.

"Holy shit," Bagget said. "Let me up."

Raider regained his feet and helped the deputy off the ground. "Sorry, Dub. I just wasn't takin' no chances."

Bagget tried to wipe the mud from his jeans. "I waited outside till you left. Norris was really mad I let you in there to see McCarty. Said he's gonna have my badge for it. What the hell was all that stuff about Red Clay Flats?"

"Come on, I'll tell you over a shot o' whiskey at Tillie's."

They started up the alley.

"You know where the judge is stayin'?" Raider asked.

"Ellrod?" Bagget replied. "He's over to Mrs. Pruitt's house."

Raider frowned. "Stayin' with the widow?"

Bagget nodded. "Stays there ever'time he comes. Pruitt and Ellrod went way back. They were Rangers together."

"Well, at least I know where t' find 'im."

"You gonna go see him?"

Raider shrugged. "I don't know what else t' do. I gotta get t' the bottom o' this an' he's the only one can help me, far as I can see."

They started up the stairs to Tillie's.

"McCarty ain't gonna get a fair trial," Bagget offered. "Hell, I come to think he's innocent. You convinced me."

"He's gonna have t' let the judge hear his case. No jury."

"Can he do that?"

Raider nodded. "I reckon he can. Wagner'll know for sure."

They knocked and Tillie let them in.

Wagner had to be awakened. The three of them talked over shots of cheap whiskey. Raider told Bagget the story about Red Clay Flats and the riders who buried Dagwood Sweeney. The deputy replied that he had heard Sweeney was working two counties over from them, and that Hand wasn't worried about him as long as he stayed out of El Paso.

Raider suggested that Hand might have had his own reasons for not worrying about Sweeney; the main reason being that he might have had foreknowledge of Sweeney's execution.

Bagget had his doubts. He didn't think his boss was capable of something like that. Hand was pretty good at keeping the peace in El Paso, but he wasn't good at much else. Not a really smart man, although he was brave and loyal.

Raider got around to suggesting that they take the evidence to Judge Ellrod. Wagner agreed that was best. He didn't think it was significant that Ellrod was staying at the widow's house. Nor did he see any trouble with fairness if McCarty argued his case before the judge. A local jury would not be as considerate as Ellrod, who would assess the facts, nothing else.

Tillie interrupted, asking if they would like coffee.

Raider saw the little wink she gave Wagner, but he didn't let on. "No coffee for these boys," the big man said. "Dub, I want you t' get Wagner back t' the hotel. Stay with 'im all night. You can sleep in a chair."

Bagget frowned. "But . . ."

"Just do it," Raider replied. "I don't want nobody hurtin' my boss."

Wagner agreed to the plan. He wanted to be away from Tillie, who held the blanket up while he dressed in his dried clothes. Did Raider suspect the tryst between him and the younger woman? It hardly seemed real to Wagner himself. He could always deny it.

His face was red when Tillie lowered the blanket. "I'm ready," he said without looking at Raider. "Shall we go, Deputy?"

Tillie complicated things by giving him a peck on the cheek. "Good-bye, William. Hope to see you soon."

Wagner turned away, his face looking like a beet. "Er, yes, thank you for your hospitality."

Raider grinned like a sour-mouthed possum. "Good night, William."

Wagner turned back, glaring at the big man.

But there was nothing for him to say.

He opened the door for Deputy Bagget. "After you, sir."

Bagget tipped his hat to Tillie. "Night, ma'am."

He started out the door.

At first Raider thought it was thunder overhead. But then Bagget slumped and fell over the railing of the stairs, thudding into the mud below. Wagner managed to step back before the second shot rang out. Raider knew immediately that it was a rifle. The slug slammed into the oven door of Tillie's stove.

The big man drew his Colt, crawling low on the floor.

"From the roof across the alley!" Wagner cried.

Raider eased back from the door. "I gotta get up there."

"You can go out the front!" Tillie cried.

Raider looked at the front window. "How far up is the roof?"

"Just a couple of feet," she replied.

Wagner was pinned against the wall. "Raider, you can't go out there!"

The rifle barked again, splintering the thin wall.

Raider crawled toward the front window. "He ain't gonna stop till we're all dead. An' nobody'll hear 'im shootin' in this rain. I gotta . . ."

Again the rifle shattered pieces of plaster and wood.

"Get him!" Wagner cried. "That's an order!"

Raider opened the window and then slid out headfirst. He sat on the sill, reaching up. Tillie had been right, it was only a couple of feet to the roof. Raider pulled himself up and hung his legs down. He dangled for a second and then rolled onto the tarred roof.

He stayed low, crawling on his belly.

It was hard to see in the rain.

The rifle barked again, firing into Tillie's place.

Raider marked the muzzle flashes. He could then see the outline of the man in the rain. One shot. Aim where he thought the chest would be. Compensate for the Colt's slight pull to the left. Squeeze the trigger gently.

The Peacemaker exploded. Raider heard the man gasp. He cried out and tried to raise the rifle toward Raider's muzzle flash. Raider rolled a few feet and fired again.

Feet scuffled on the other roof. The man came to the edge, holding his chest. He gaped at Raider, like he was trying to see the man who had killed him. Then he fell forward, crashing to the ground where Deputy Bagget lay bleeding in the mud.

Raider rolled his legs off the roof, hanging in front of Tillie's door, dropping to the landing at the top of the stairs.

Wagner peered out at him. "Good work, man."

"Come on, let's go look at the damage."

They hurried down to Bagget's side. Raider lifted his face from the mud. A huge hole had been opened in the middle of his forehead. Raider let him fall back into the mud.

"Gone."

Wagner frowned. "My God!"

Raider hovered over the body of Bagget's killer.

"Is it Hand?" Wagner asked.

Raider shook his head. "Don't rec'nize 'im. But I'm bettin' he's seen us afore. Prob'ly t'day."

Wagner gawked at the big man. "What are you talking about?"

"Look at 'is boots," Raider replied. "Covered with red clay, just like mine. He was at the flats t'day."

"You think he was one of the men who buried the body?"

Raider nodded. "Yep. Prob'ly the one who wanted t' follow our tracks."

"But how could he find us in all that rain?"

"Easy," Raider said, "doubled back on his own. Spotted us diggin' up Sweeney. Then trailed us here. He knew we were headin' t' El Paso. Probably followed you an' set up t' wait for us. Bagget was just unlucky that this one decided to shoot when he did."

Lightning flashed overhead.

Raider looked up at Wagner. "What now, Boss?"

Wagner was dubious. "Well, the proper thing to do would be to go straight to the sheriff."

"Yeah," Raider said disgustedly.

"Three dead men in one day," Wagner replied. "Not good."

"Nope. Not good at all."

Wagner then said they should go straight to Judge Ellrod.

Raider replied that for once, they were both in complete agreement on something.

FIFTEEN

Raider loaded the two bodies onto Wagner's mare. They led her through the back alleys, making for Pruitt's house. When Raider saw the glow of the lights through the rain, he stopped Wagner and handed him the reins of the mare.

"Stay here."

Wagner startled a little. "But . . ."

"Just gonna have a look," the big man grunted. "Maybe the judge is in trouble too. This thing gets bigger all the time."

"Be careful."

Raider asked him if he had the derringer. When Wagner replied that he had his hand on the tiny weapon, Raider started off into the shadows. Wagner shivered until the big man returned.

"What?" Wagner asked.

Raider took the reins from him. "They're havin' coffee. Ever'thin' looks t' be fine. We'll wait till the lights go out in the parlor. I don't want t' disturb the lady."

Despite Wagner's grousing to the contrary, they huddled under the ragged awning of a printing company across the street from Mrs. Pruitt's place. Raider had swung around behind the house on his reconnaisance run. The widow Pruitt had a nice back barnyard, complete with stables and a pen for the milk cow. Maybe a place for them to sleep if the gunplay got too hot.

"There," Wagner said finally, "the lights are out in the parlor."

"One more minute. Okay, the lamp is on upstairs. Let's hope the judge will come t' the back door."

They hurried as fast as the mare would go with the two dead men on her back.

Raider knocked for a long time before the light of an oil lamp swelled in the windows of the kitchen.

"Who is it?"

"It's Raider, Judge."

"Who?"

Wagner stepped up to the door. "It's William Wagner, Judge Ellrod. You remember me. From the stagecoach. And you were there when I got Raider out of jail. Remember, we were almost robbed and . . ."

The door swung open. Ellrod hung his head out into the rain. Raider nodded, marking the pistol in the judge's hand. It was a pocket revolver, like the one Tillie had brought Raider in her aborted escape plan.

Ellrod glared at them with his grey eyes. "Don't you gentlemen know the hour? And there's a lady in the house!"

"You're gonna want t' hear what we have t' say," Raider offered. "I brought you a couple a house guests."

Ellrod looked over their shoulders, gaping at the pair of dead men on the mare's back. "My God. What is this?"

Raider shook his head. "We ain't rightly sure. But we're ass-deep in it. That one there killed the deputy and then I killed him. It's got somethin' t' do with Pruitt's death an' a place called Red Clay Flats."

Ellrod's face went white. "Come in. My word. Murders."

"What about the bodies?" Raider asked.

Ellrod gestured with the revolver. "Lay them on the ground. Cover them with the blanket from your horse. Then come in out of the rain. I want to hear everything."

After the bodies were spread out and covered up, Raider and Wagner went into the kitchen of the widow's house. Ellrod got them some hot coffee and flavored it with good brandy.

When the judge sat down at the table with them, Raider began to talk.

"First off, the Kid ain't guilty of killin' Pruitt. I'm sure o' that. Pruitt's death has somethin' t' do with the goin's on at Red Clay Flats. Wagner an' I were out there today."

Ellrod's trembling hand lifted the coffee cup to his lips. "You aren't making yourself clear, Raider. I don't even know what Red Clay Flats is."

"A barren stretch of ground," Wagner chimed in. "And

somebody is burying bodies out there. Raider and I identified one Dagwood Sweeney, a criminal of little notoriety, but still a convict and a blackguard."

Ellrod shook his head. "Never heard of Sweeney. You say you *saw* these men bury this dead man?"

Raider nodded. "I figure they knew we saw 'em too, or at least one of 'em did. That one I killed had red clay all over 'is boots. I think he wanted t' follow our tracks all along, but nobody else wanted to. He doubled back an' picked up our trail. Probably saw us and held back where we weren't lookin'. Got set, when he followed Wagner home, an' waited. Got the deputy when he opened the door. Poor Bagget. I think he was a good man. Not involved in any of Hand's doin's."

Ellrod flashed grey irises at the big man. "You really think Hand is involved in this?"

Raider shrugged. "It points to it. He refused t' listen when I say the Kid isn't guilty. Bonn . . . McCarty just got caught at the wrong place at the wrong time. Hand was layin' for 'im. It just smells like a frame t' me."

Ellrod grimaced, leaning back. "Except for one thing. When Norris Hand received the note tipping him on the whereabouts of Pruitt's body, Mrs. Pruitt happened to be with her brother. She saw the note. It really was an anonymous message that tipped the sheriff."

"Maybe Hand had the note sent to himself," Wagner offered.

Ellrod nodded. "Maybe."

"I think Pruitt knew about the goin's on at Red Clay Flats," Raider offered. "That's why he was killed."

The judge eyed the big man. "What do you think is going on out there, Raider?"

A sigh from the tall Pinkerton agent. "I don't rightly know. Maybe some gang is usin' the Flats for a place t' plant them they got grudges against. Those four could've been Sweeney's compadres. Maybe he just crossed 'em."

"But you seem to think there's more than one man buried out there," Ellrod said. "Don't you?"

He nodded. "Yeah. My nose told me there was. My horse smelled it too. We'd have t' go out there an' dig around if we wanted t' make sure. I could be wrong. It's happened before."

The judge leaned back, pouring more brandy into his coffee cup. After he drank, he frowned at them. "Gents, I don't know what you've stumbled into here. It doesn't sound good. I'm not sure what I can do about it. My jurisdiction in the matter might be limited. Do you think Norris Hand has anything to do with the burials on Red Clay Flats?"

Raider exhaled. "Funny, when I dropped it on him, he didn't flinch. He could be that cool. Or maybe he's just a pawn. Doesn't know he's bein' jerked around. I've seen that afore, too."

Ellrod stood up, looking older and tireder. "Give me a couple of days, gentlemen. I'll go all the way to the governor if I have to.

Raider and Wagner got up as well.

The big man tipped back his Stetson. "Judge, you might want t' ask round, check with the nearest marshal. See if there's been a boy named of Murph Hizer ridin' in these parts."

Wagner gaped at his ne'er-do-well partner. "Where did you come up with that name?"

"Never mind. Just ask, Judge. See what it turns up."

Ellrod nodded, urging them toward the door. "You've done a fine job, men. I commend you. I'll let you know if I need you for anything else."

"What about those bodies?" Wagner asked.

Ellrod frowned. "Best to keep that quiet for as long as possible. I don't want the town to get word that one of their deputies has been killed. It might make unrest."

Raider looked at the lawman. "Gotta agree with you there, Judge. Don't want no lynchin' party."

"I don't understand," Wagner said.

"The town might blame the kid in jail," Raider replied. "'Specially if Bagget was a popular law officer. McCarty might be a good target for 'em if they decide t' avenge the deputy."

Ellrod smiled at the big Pinkerton. "Like I said, you can always come to work for me, Raider. You have a good head for figuring things."

"I wish I could agree with you, Judge. For the life of me, I can't put all this in one basket and make it come out eggs. The bodies keep pilin' up an' so far I ain't been able t' do anythin' t' stop it."

"We'll get it stopped," the Judge urged. "But for now, you got to sit tight and let me take care of this. You might even think about taking your leave and finishing up your business in Arizona. I can call in the marshal when I get to the bottom of things."

"We'll hang round," Raider said. "Ain't that right, Wagner?"

Wagner nodded. "We'll be happy to give you a hand until the marshal arrives."

Ellrod clapped him on the back. "Glad I can count on you, men."

"If we want t' see you, we'll come at night," Raider offered. "No need t' let on t' the whole town that we're workin' t'gether. Might be some o' the city fathers in on all this. Whatever the hell it is."

Ellrod agreed to operate in secrecy. He urged them again to give him time to call in more help. At least a couple of days.

The judge grimaced when he saw the bodies. "Damn, I hate this kind of thing. It just irks my craw."

Raider stepped out into the drizzle and lifted the blanket from the bodies. "Want me t' put 'em in the stable there? Cover 'em with straw?"

"I'll do it," Ellrod said quickly.

"No trouble, Judge."

Ellrod waved him off. "No, Raider, you and Wagner look like you could use some rest. I'll take care of it. Meanwhile, you boys head home. Make sure nobody follows you."

Wagner frowned at Ellrod. "You're just going to leave those two men in the stable?"

"Until I can get the undertaker up here," the judge replied. "Probably have to pay him extra to keep him quiet. I wonder if Bagget had any kin? They'll have to be told sooner or later."

"Tell 'em later," Raider offered. "Come on, William. Let's follow the judge's advice an' go home."

"Back to Tillie's?" Wagner asked.

Raider grabbed the reins of the mare and started through the shadows. "You can do what you want, Wagner. I'm goin' back t' make sure Tillie's all right. She's probably scared half t' death."

Wagner fell in, trying to match the big man's stride. "Well, the judge was helpful. I suppose we're almost finished here."

They trudged across the muddy street. "Ain't leavin' till the Kid is outta jail," Raider replied. "That's what I said I'd do and I aim t' do it."

"You mean Billy the Kid?"

Raider stopped and glared over his shoulder. "Why'd you say that?"

Wagner snorted triumphantly. "Ha. So it's true."

"You figured it out, then?"

"You've made several slips of the tongue," Wagner replied. "You've called him Billy and several times you almost slipped out with another name. You've had to think about his name every time you called him McCarty. Most often you have called him, 'the Kid,' which I took to be a sure sign that he was someone other than Henry McCarty."

Raider turned back toward the alley, resuming his stride. "So you know. What are you gonna do 'bout it?"

Wagner followed him, trying to keep up. "Well, he really hasn't done anything wrong here."

"He didn't kill Pruitt, anyways."

Wagner didn't like the sound of that. "You think he might be part of the thing on Red Clay Flats?"

Raider shrugged, slipping into a passageway between two buildings. "Don't know. That name Murph Hizer was give t' me by the Kid. Billy used t' ride with a gun-for-hire gang called the Regulators."

Wagner nodded, following the big man. "I know. Up in Lincoln County. We were asked to come into that, but it was too messy."

Raider grunted. "Probably woulda sent me up there if you hadn't."

They walked through the rain, not saying another word until they reached Tillie's place.

Wagner told Raider to take the mare back to the livery.

The big man nodded, but then looked at his boss. "What about the Kid? You gonna tell the judge who he really is?"

"No. Not unless it's absolutely necessary. And then, only if the boy had something to do with Pruitt's murder or the debacle at Red Clay Flats."

Raider tried to smile. "You're a good man, Wagner. I don't care what anybody else says. You're all right."

"Just be patient," Wagner offered. "Try to go along with

the judge. See it through until the marshals arrive. Until then, just try to stay out of trouble."

Raider said he'd do his best.

That night, in an awkward arrangement, Raider and Wagner slept on the floor while Tillie slept in her own bed.

They woke early the next day to the smell of a big breakfast: ham and eggs, biscuits and redeye gravy. While they were eating, Tillie told them they had to fix her walls where the bullets had ripped through. She was going to order tools and lumber from a man she knew.

Wagner asked her to send a message for him at the telegraph office. He wrote it down and she agreed to drop it off. Raider told her to check and see if the judge had sent any messages out, say to Austin or San Antonio. He might have to go that far to get all the marshals he was going to need.

Tillie left and came back an hour later with the lumberman behind her. While he unloaded his buckboard Tillie told Wagner that the judge had issued an order that the telegraph office should be closed for one week. Norris Hand was backing up the order.

Raider started to sweat. "Don't like the sound o' that, William."

Wagner did not know what to think. "Maybe Ellrod is waiting for the marshals to come."

"Let's hope so."

They went to work, sawing, hammering, nailing.

Tillie was delighted by the repairs, saying how the cold January wind would have howled through all those holes.

When they were finished, Raider looked at the leftover lumber. He started to work frantically, fashioning a crude ladder. Raising the ladder to the edge of the roof from the landing at the top of Tillie's stairs, he climbed up to the roof and motioned for Wagner to hand him the one long board that remained. Wagner did not know what the big man was doing, and he grumbled as he handed up the board. Raider seemed to be wasting time.

Raider motioned for him to come up the ladder. Wagner protested but finally ascended to see what the big man wanted. Raider showed him how the long board stretched over the alley to the next roof. They could walk across, spanning each space between the buildings until they were all the way to the street.

"We can watch everything that goes on at the sheriff's office an' on the main street," he offered to his boss.

Wagner wiped his forehead in the heat. "Good idea."

"You take the first watch," Raider said, heading for the ladder.

"But . . ."

"Just do it," Raider said. "I'll relieve you at dark."

"That's almost three hours away!"

Raider smiled. "You don't have t' thank me."

"Raider?"

The big man looked over the first rung of the ladder. "Yeah?"

Wagner sighed and looked toward the street. "I don't like the idea of the telegraph office being closed."

"Neither do I, Boss."

"We'll go see the judge tonight."

Raider nodded. "You keep an eye on things."

They agreed to meet again in an hour.

Raider went down to clean up the mess from the repairs.

Tillie came past him on the stairs, a towel draped over her shoulder.

He gawked at her. "Where you goin'?"

She shrugged demurely. "It's already a hot day," she said. "I thought I might go take a bath. There's a tub downstairs in the warehouse. Want to come along?" She ran her fingers over his chest. "You're so hot and sweaty."

Raider waved her off. "Better not. Not with Wagner sneakin' round."

"Wagner's not as innocent as you think."

He glared at her, pointing a finger. "Look here, Tillie. You don't let on like I know."

She grinned. "Know what?"

"What you and Wagner did."

She winked. "I thought you'd want me to."

He sighed. "Tillie, I ain't never met a woman I like more'n I like you. You're sweet, you don't complain, an' you got a good notion of what a man wants t' do in bed. But this case is gettin' crazier ever' minute. Maybe you better go someplace else for a while so you don't get hurt."

She kissed him on the cheek and laughed. "I won't get hurt. And nobody is going to make me leave my house. I'm a seamstress, remember?"

He thought again about a cool bath. Better not, as long as Wagner was on the roof. He knew he'd lose Tillie as soon as the Kid was free. A woman in love stayed with her man, even if he was a punk.

"See you later, Raider. Hey, that rhymes."

She went down the stairs and entered the warehouse below through a side door.

Raider took a step and felt the nail going through the sole of his boot. It didn't break the skin, but it still gave him a sharp pain. He pulled it out and went back to work.

The lumberman had also brought some whitewash, so Raider mixed it up with water and painted over the new wood.

"Not bad," said the voice from above.

Raider looked up to see Wagner staring down at him. "See anything int'restin'?" the big man asked.

Wagner squinted. "Nothing too exciting. Norris Hand has a new deputy. Rugged looking fellow. I think Hand knows Bagget is dead, otherwise he wouldn't have hired a new man."

"Makes sense. You wanna changes places with me? Clean up some o' this mess down here?"

Wagner drew back. "Uh, actually I think I prefer surveillance. Call me when you're finished."

"Why you . . ."

But then the big man had to laugh. At least his boss was developing a sense of humor. He thought Wagner might need it for what lay ahead.

Why the hell had Ellrod closed the damned telegraph office? That wasn't necessary. Maybe Hand had forced the judge to do it. Raider decided that he would send Wagner for help if the sheriff had Ellrod under his control.

Ellrod had seemed so sure of himself. Maybe he was blinded because his old friend had been killed. Maybe he was acting in haste to get to the men who had murdered his compadre.

"Ow. . ."

He looked down at a splinter in his thumb.

"Deep, damn it."

He was trying to pick it out when Tillie came out of the

warehouse. Her hair was wet and she now wore a white robe. She saw him as she walked up the stairs.

"You tryin' to bite your thumb off?"

Raider took the wounded digit out of his mouth. "It hurts."

"Let me fix it."

Inside, she dug it out with a needle. Raider flinched when she poured a tincture on the cut. She wrapped it with a piece of cotton cloth.

"You need a bath," she said. "I left you water in the tub."

Raider said that was nice of her. He had to get out in a hurry. The smell of a bath-sweet woman was almost too much for him.

Downstairs in the warehouse, he stripped and got into the tub.

He half expected Tillie to join him, but she never came. So he washed and sat for a while in the cool water. He tried to think about everything that had happened. Why did all the pieces seem so different? Usually in a case there was a common thread. But this one had too many loose ends.

Nothing to do but get out of the tub, towel off, and go back upstairs.

Tillie was putting everything in order. Her hair was dry now and she had combed it out. Raider had to fight that scent of her body.

"Y'all did a good job," she said.

She was still wearing the robe.

Raider grunted. "We did okay. I'm just sorry you had t' . . ."

She kissed him.

That was all it took.

Raider embraced her, pressing his mouth to hers, running his hands inside her robe.

Tillie untied the sash, pressing her body against his. He lowered his mouth to her nipples, suckling her firm breasts. She ran her hands down his knotty stomach, reaching for the buttons of his jeans.

Raider cupped her backside, picking her up, carrying her to the bed.

Her hands freed the massive thickness of his manhood. She spread her legs as she fell back on the bedcover. Raider guided his shaft to the glistening wetness of her cunt.

He entered and finished quickly.

Tillie seemed to have her fill, despite his hasty climax. She guided his head to her chest and told him to suckle her. That was all she wanted. She didn't care about anything anymore. She had even given up on seeing Billy again. Raider tried to tell her that Billy would be freed, but she only pulled him back to her breasts.

It was quiet for a while. They lay in the heat of late afternoon, gradually drifting off to sleep. When they were awakened, it was almost dark and Wagner was shouting from the roof.

"Keep your shirt on," Raider called back. "I'll come up."

"What is it?" Tillie asked.

"It's my turn t' watch the street."

"Raider! Come out here."

The big man pulled up his pants and stuck his head out the door. "What the devil is wrong with you, Wagner?"

"You've got to come quickly," he said. "I think there's going to be trouble. Hurry."

Raider scurried up the ladder in his bare feet. They walked across the board from roof to roof until they were facing the street. At first glance, it appeared that everything was calm.

"I don't see no trouble, Wagner. Hell, if you wanted me to stand watch, you didn't have t' . . ."

"No," Wagner insisted, "Listen to me. For the past hour, men have been running toward that section of town."

He pointed to the north.

Raider peered across the rooftops, making out a glow in the same area of town where the judge was staying. "Torches," he said. "Shit. I hope the judge ain't in trouble."

Raider started to turn away, ready to pick up his weapons and go see Ellrod.

Wagner cried out. "Look! It's moving."

Sure enough, the glow of the torches had started to move south, working a path through the side streets.

Raider watched as the torches became more visible, along with the men who carried them. "Funny thing about a lynch mob," he said, "you can usually hear 'em long afore you see 'em. If you ain't lookin' from up here, anyway."

"How?" Wagner asked.

"Maybe the undertaker got word out," Raider replied. "The

judge had t' do somethin' with those bodies. Now that they know Bagget is dead, they're gonna get revenge on the Kid. They probably believe the Kid had somethin' t' do with Bagget's death. An' hell, who knows, maybe he did. Murph Hizer used t' ride with Billy. Maybe this whole thing is just the opposite of how we been seein' it."

Wagner had turned white. "Good Lord."

Raider started back across the roof tops. "Come on, Boss. We got work t' do."

Wagner followed the big man. "What can we do? We're just two against a whole army of men. Damn it, I'd sure like to know who told them Bagget was dead. I'd like to wring his neck!"

Raider walked over the board to the next rooftop, turning when he had crossed to steady the board for Wagner. "Don't fret, William. We'll take it one step at a time."

Wagner walked across the board. "What do you want me to do?" he asked on the other side.

"Go tell Norris Hand there's a lynch mob comin' an' then get the hell outta there. Come back t' Tillie's an' wait for me."

"But . . ."

"Just do it."

"And what will you do?" Wagner asked.

"I'm gonna free the Kid," Raider replied. "An' then we're all gonna get some answers."

SIXTEEN

By the time Wagner climbed down the ladder, Raider was on the grey, galloping toward the jailhouse. Wagner had wondered why the big man had seen fit to get the grey from the stable when he returned the mare to the livery. Always have a fresh horse ready, Raider had said. A good rule to follow.

Wagner stuck his head in the door. "Tillie. Do be a good girl and sit tight. There's going to be a lot of trouble."

"Don't worry about me," came the reply. "I'll shoot anyone that tries to mess with me."

Wagner believed her. He turned and hurried down the stairs, running through the alley as fast as his aging legs would carry him. He was beginning to appreciate the great amount of physical effort it took to solve a case. Not that this affair was really a true case. He had not even notified Allan Pinkerton that they were assisting Judge Ellrod.

What would the strict Scotsman say about Wagner working on his own?

Wasn't he an authority in the agency?

Didn't Wagner have a right to take a case on his own judgment?

It had all happened so fast, he thought as he turned into the street. Raider had a way of pulling things along. The big man had gotten them this far on his balls alone. Gotten them right into trouble.

He could hear the echo of the mob, faint and steady like the far off roll of threatening thunder.

Lights were burning in the sheriff's office. Wagner banged hard on the door until the new deputy answered. He didn't look as smart as Bagget.

"Whut?"

Wagner pointed toward the north. "There's a lynch mob on

he way to hang that boy you've got locked up."

The new deputy smiled dumbly. "Sheeit. You're out of our noggin', ol' man. Git outta here an' . . ."

A high-pitched shout resounded through the street.

The sound froze both of them.

"I saw them," Wagner insisted. "They'll be here in a hurry. Where the hell is Sheriff Hand? He's the only one who can top them."

"I ain't seen 'im since this mornin'," the new deputy replied. "He jest put me in charge an' took off with that judge."

Wagner started to say something, but the torches turned a orner, sliding onto the main street.

The new deputy broke away from the jailhouse door, runing headlong in the other direction.

Wagner stared helplessly at the mob as they stormed up the treet. There must have been fifty torches, with two men for ach torch. How was he going to dissuade a hundred men that hey shouldn't hang the Kid who rested in the El Paso jail?

When the mob reached the sheriff's office, they stopped to ook at Wagner.

The white-faced little man held up his arms. "You can't do his!" he cried. "Please!"

Someone shouted from the pack: "Who the hell is he?"

"That Pinkerton," someone replied.

"One of that kid's men killed Bagget!" another man houted.

A cheer of agreement from the crowd.

Someone pointed a finger at Wagner. "Our truck ain't with ou, Pink. Just step aside and we won't hurt you."

"We will not be denied our vengeance!"

Another loud cry from the group.

He would have to step aside. Let them have the Kid. Billy he Kid.

The crowd surged forward.

Wagner pressed against the wall, waiting for them to go ast him.

But then the jailhouse seemed to shake, to tremble like it vas in the middle of an earthquake.

"Raider," Wagner said under his breath.

He knew then that the mob had gotten there too late.

• • •

Raider took the shortest route to the back of the jailhouse He had to ride through a couple of alleys before he saw th barred windows in the evening shadows. He knew the alle from the hours he had spent staring out of his own cell win dow while he was in stir. He also knew that the bars of the ce had been set in cheap adobe plaster.

Jumping down from the grey, he ran up to the set of bar on the right. "Kid," he called. "Kid, come to the window! Ge your face up here."

Billy leered out into the shadows. "Pinkerton?"

Raider urged him to sit tight. He went back to the grey an got the rope from the saddle. Billy didn't have to be told. H caught the rope and tied it around the bars.

Raider climbed onto the grey and tied the rope to the saddl horn. "Push from your side, Billy." He patted the grey. "Let' see how much you got left, boy."

He spurred the animal and the rope tightened.

The bars came loose on the first try, without a hitch. I made the building shake. Billy started to climb out of the hol in the wall.

"What's all that noise?" he asked as he leapt onto the grey riding double with Raider.

"Your funeral if we don't get outta here."

"Then ride, Pink-man!"

Raider guided the grey through the back streets, windin away from the disappointed lynch mob. He wondered i Wagner had gotten out of there in time. He sure hoped hi boss hadn't been hurt in the melee.

"Where we goin'?" asked William Bonney.

"Someplace close," Raider replied.

Bonney let out an exasperated breath. "Damn you, Pink Why don't we just dig for New Mexico?'

The big man did not reply. He broke away from the alleys driving straight down main street for the widow Pruitt's. H planned to leave Bonney with the judge. Maybe Billy the Ki would be safe there.

He felt a hand coming around him, reaching for his Colt.

Raider reined up, stopping hard. He swung his right elbov around, knocking the Kid from his saddle. Billy hit the groun on his back, sucking for the breath that had left him on im pact.

Raider glared down at him from the saddle. "Billy, I didn't break you out so you could run off again. You're gonna see this through. I don't know if you noticed or not, but I ain't the kinda man you mess with. You may be hot shit up there in Lincoln County, but right now you're just another punk that got hisself in trouble."

Billy coughed, holding his chest.

Raider drew his Colt. "You hear me, Billy?"

The Kid nodded.

A loud roar echoed behind them.

"Your necktie party is still lookin' for you," the big man offered. "You wanna hang around?"

Billy leered at him. "That ain't funny, Pinkerton. Hell, I think you broke my damned back."

"Come on."

Billy ran alongside the grey until they entered the barnyard of the widow Pruitt's house. Raider climbed down, keeping his Peacemaker in hand. He gave the reins to Billy.

"Let's hide in the stable for now."

Billy frowned. "Come on, Pink, let me go. I'll pay you. I got money back in New Mexico. Come with me."

Raider waved the barrel of the Peacemaker. "Come on, Billy. In the stable. Those madmen may come lookin' for the judge."

William Bonney reluctantly led the grey into the stable.

Raider came behind him in the shadows. They sat in the dark, listening, as the lynch mob arrived at the house of the widow Pruitt. For a moment. Raider thought they might burn the place down. A mob hungered for some sort of vengeance. But Raider heard the judge's voice and the mob slowly dispersed.

He looked at the Kid, who was rolling a cigarette. "Well, that's one thing in our favor."

"Let me go, Pinkerton. Hell, I ain't done nothin' to you."

Raider sighed, shaking his head. "Wouldn't it mean more t' you if you was free an' clear with the law?"

Billy shrugged. 'I been in so much trouble, mister, it don't rightly matter what the law thinks of me."

He licked the paper of the cigarette.

"I've always held smokin' to be an unhealthful practice," Raider offered.

The Kid struck a match. "To hell with you then."

A circle of light flared up with the match.

Billy saw Raider's eyes bulge. He held the match in front of him. "What is it?"

"Behind you," Raider said.

The match burned Billy's fingers and he dropped it on the ground.

"Strike another one."

Billy obeyed him, wondering what the hell was going on. "Somebody sneakin' up behind me?"

But Raider was staring at one of the mounts in the stable. Billy looked at it too. He said it resembled the pinto Murph Hizer used to ride. The Pinkerton seemed to be more interested in the horse's hooves. Bonney didn't catch on until it was explained to him by the big man. Then he understood perfectly and he had to smile at the way Raider had put it all together so quickly.

When the lynch mob was gone, Wagner staggered back across the street. He returned to Tillie's. The girl was sitting calmly on her bed, knitting. She said hello to him, seemingly uninterested in the goings-on at the sheriff's office.

Wagner felt drained, but he knew he had to climb back onto the roof.

When he was at the edge of the main street overlook, he peered in the direction of the lynch mob as it thundered toward the widow Pruitt's house.

What the devil did they want there? To see the judge? Surely they didn't intend to hang Ellrod. Did they think he would know where Raider took the Kid? It was all so flabbergasting.

He breathed easier when the mob dispersed. Now everyone was safe for the time being. He kept watch for a while, but then decided there was nothing he could do. Raider had acted so quickly. There hadn't been time to complete the plan. So far it had been an effective ploy, even if Wagner didn't know what the next move would be.

He went back down to Tillie's.

"You want some soup?" she asked as he came in.

"How about some liquor?"

She poured cheap whiskey for him. "You look frazzled," she offered.

Wagner laughed until he began to cry.

Tillie put a hand on his shoulder. "Hey, what happened out there?"

He composed himself and told her about the lynch mob.

Tillie looked uneasy as she poured him another drink.

Wagner eyed her suspiciously. "Tillie, do you know something you're not telling me?"

She shook her head. "I'm just worried about Billy . . . I mean Henry."

Wagner smiled weakly. "I know about William Bonney," he replied.

"Raider told you?"

"I figured it out myself."

She frowned. "What are you goin' to do?"

"What can I do?" he offered. "Except sit here and wait for Raider to get word to me."

"I sure hope Billy is all right."

Wagner assured her that he was. Raider had made a clean getaway. They would show up sooner or later.

Tillie put a hand to her throat. "I sure hope so."

"Are you quite all right?" Wagner asked her.

She nodded. "Yes. I just got a bad feelin'."

He told her not to be superstitious.

"I just feel like it ain't even close to bein' over for Billy and Raider. I don't know why, but I just do."

Wagner prayed the girl was wrong.

SEVENTEEN

Raider walked through the barnyard with Billy the Kid trailing in his footsteps. He had not tied the Kid's hands, anticipating the need for some extra help, especially if things fell the way he thought they would. Billy had asked for a gun and the big man had almost given it to him. Finally he had settled on leaving the Kid's hands free.

A light burned in the kitchen of the Pruitt house. Raider eased up to the window, staring in. Nobody at the table. He motioned for Billy to come closer.

Bonney had agreed to cooperate after the tall Pinkerton had laid it out for him. "Anybody home, Pink-man?"

Raider reached for the doorknob. "I reckon it's time t' find out."

He pushed through the doorway, his gun hand resting on the butt of his Peacemaker. The kitchen was warm. Somebody had been cooking on the wood stove. The widow Pruitt. Raider wondered if she had anything to do with it.

"Nobody here," Billy offered. "Guess we'll . . ."

A shape appeared in the frame of the kitchen archway.

Raider drew the Colt and thumbed the hammer. "Don't move."

Billy whistled. "Fast, Pink-man. But not as fast as me."

"Shut up, Kid."

The shape moved into the light.

Judge Ellrod glared at the bore of the Colt. "Raider! What the devil are you doing?"

The big man held the .45 still. "Who's here with you, Judge?"

Ellrod frowned. "No one. Just the widow. Raider, I don't see the need for that weapon."

Billy sat down at the kitchen table. "I'm hungry."

Ellrod noticed him for the first time. "McCarty! What are you doing here? How did you get out of jail?"

Bonney threw out his hands. "Big 'un here sprung me when the lynch mob came after my hide. You should know, Judge. You turned 'em away."

Raider eyed the older man. "That's right, Judge. You talked sense into that bunch. Like you was their leader."

Ellrod started toward the table. "But I . . ."

Raider stopped him. "Don't sit down yet, Judge. Not till you've done some talkin'."

Ellrod seemed to relax. "All right. I don't need this impertinence, but if I must go along with it . . . of course, let me remind you that you are in conflict with the law, Raider. Having broken McCarty here out of jail."

"I saved 'is life," the big man replied. "Somebody set him up twice. First with Norris Hand, then with that lynch mob."

Billy winked at the judge. "That's right, Ellrod. You listen to this man. He knows what he's doin'."

Ellrod had begun to tremble. "I couldn't help what happened with that mob. I told the undertaker to keep quiet, but he had to shoot his mouth off. He's the one who stirred them up!"

"Then why'd they come back t' you?" Raider asked. "Why'd they start in this part o' town? Why'd you close the telegraph office?"

Billy laughed. "He's got you there, Judge."

"I'll see that both of you hang!" Ellrod cried.

The Kid exhaled disgustedly. "You're a shallow individual, Judge."

Raider shot a dirty look at the Kid. "You can stop runnin' your mouth any time, boy."

"'Scuse me."

He looked back at the Judge. "Answer my questions, Ellrod. Why'd you seal things off an' try t' get that mob stirred up?"

"I did no such thing!"

Raider chortled. "I never would've thought twice 'bout everythin' till I saw that pinto in your stable. Where'd it come from?"

Ellrod looked away, hiding his grey eyes. "I don't know what you're talking about."

"That pinto has fresh red clay on its hooves, Judge. It's been out t' Red Clay Flats in the last couple a days. I'm guessin' it was rode by the one that killed Bagget, the boy that ambushed us after we was out there. Would that be right, Judge?"

Ellrod remained silent.

Billy laughed again. "You know the funny thing of it, Judge? Raider here never woulda seen them hooves with the red clay if I hadn't lit up a cigarette. Hell, he'd be in here trusting you and spillin' his guts. He ain't learned not to trust a lawman. Not yet, anyway."

Ellrod bared his teeth at Bonney. "I thought he told you to shut your damned mouth."

"Oooh," Billy replied. "Touchy. Y' know somethin', Raider, I think he's guilty."

Raider looked at Billy. "You ain't off the hook yourself, Kid. You still gotta answer what you know 'bout Murph Hizer."

"Aw, Murph Hizer's probably the one you killed," Bonney said. "I'll bet he's six feet under."

"I'll bet he isn't," the judge replied with a smile. "In fact, I'd bet he's standing right behind you with a gun drawn."

Raider kept his eyes locked on the judge. "You're bluffin'."

Billy looked around instead. "No he ain't, Raider."

The big man from Arkansas heard the clicking hammer behind him.

"Drop that gun, Pinkerton. Or I'll drop you."

The voice was rough, like a cat's tongue.

Raider held steady on Ellrod. "I'll kill your boss if you take me."

Ellrod looked sympathetically at the Colt. "Raider, you're a good man. Don't make him kill you."

Billy gaped at the big Remington .44 in Murph Hizer's hand. "Hi there, Murph. You gonna let me go?"

Hizer had a grizzled face, leering eyes, dirty teeth. "Howdy, Kid. Gee, I'd like to let you go. But you're with the Pinkerton here."

Billy shrugged. "Ain't necessarily with him. Course, I don't know how proud you can be, Murph. I mean, you are with the judge. If that ain't walkin' the other side of the law, I don't know what is."

That seemed to confuse Hizer, but he still held the Remington on Raider. "Come on, big 'un. Drop it."

"I can use you, Raider," the judge offered. "Please. I don't want to see you dead."

Raider's eyes narrowed. "Then you *are* behind all this. Even the thing on Red Clay Flats."

"Don't you see," Ellrod said. "There's not enough law to go around. I can try some of the outlaws and I can hang most of the ones I sentence. But some won't quit, even after they've been in prison. There's got to be another way."

Raider sighed. "So you hired some of the Regulators. Including Billy here. Is that what you did to make your own law?"

Bonney turned back to the big man. "Whoa, Raider. I ain't never rode for this man. I don't know him."

"Who was the one I killed?" Raider asked.

"Turk Simpson," replied Murph Hizer. "He was the one who thought somebody had been out on the Flats nosin' around. I loaned him my pinto so he could ride back to take a look."

Ellrod focused his grey irises on Raider's face. "Join us. You can do much more good than you could working for Pinkerton."

Raider scowled at the judge. "You mean go out and round up men like Dagwood Sweeney and plant 'em without a trial or a jury?"

"Sweeney was beyond redemption," Ellrod replied. "Prison did nothing for him. As soon as he was out, he went right back to robbing and killing. I simply saved the state some money and trouble by doing away with him."

"How many you got planted out there?" Billy asked.

Ellrod ignored him. "Raider, don't be foolish. You're too good to waste with a bullet. Look how quickly you got onto me. With ability like that working for us, we won't need to hire the likes of him."

Hizer bristled. "Hey, don't talk like that."

Raider looked sideways to see the Remington staring back with one cold black eye. It would be a standoff. He might plug the judge, or he might wheel and get off a round at Hizer.

One thing for sure—Hizer would get off his shot and he probably wouldn't miss.

The judge ignored his unsavory associate. "Raider, toss the gun on the floor. We don't need this."

Raider felt the sweat breaking on his forehead. "You're just gonna kill me anyway, Judge. Ain't that right?"

Ellrod tried to smile. "Not necessarily."

"Don't trust him, Raider!" the Kid cried. "He's a stinkin' lawman!"

But there wasn't much else to do. Raider figured he could at least play along with Ellrod until he saw a chance for a break. He had to gamble that the judge really meant what he said about hiring him.

"All right, Judge," the big man said. "You win. If I drop the gun, you won't kill me?"

"No. Not if you'll listen to what I have to say."

"Okay."

Raider looked back at Hizer.

"I'm droppin' the Colt, boy. Don't shoot. I'm gonna throw it right there on the floor."

Hizer nodded. "Okay, but . . ."

Raider threw the Peacemaker into the air.

They were all surprised by what happened next.

Raider had never seen anyone move so fast.

Before the gun hit the floor, William Bonney had kicked back from the table. When the chair slammed down, he rolled and reached for the pistol. He caught it in mid-air and came up shooting, firing two slugs straight into the chest of a gawking Murph Hizer. Hizer stumbled backward and fell against the kitchen wall.

Hizer vomited a stream of blood.

"Sorry, Murph," said Billy the Kid. "But you asked for it."

The outlaw fell forward into a pool of his own fluid.

Raider started to move toward the Kid.

Billy thumbed the hammer of the Peacemaker. "Don't make me do it, Raider. I don't want to kill you."

Ellrod was inching back toward the archway.

"Stay still, Judge," the Kid urged. "We got to figure this out."

Raider looked down the barrel of his own pistol. "Fancy moves, Kid. Now give me back my gun."

Billy stopped him with a gesture. "Please, big man. I kinda got to like you back there when we was in jail. And I won't forget how you broke me out and saved me from that mob. But I got to get a move on. And I have to kill anybody who tries to stop me.'

"You'll get a fair trial," Raider offered.

Billy just laughed, shaking his head. "Ain't nobody gonna be fair to William Bonney. But hell, don't fret. You still caught the judge here. He's runnin' his own brand of the law on this herd. And even after I'm gone, I'm sure you'll be able to prove he killed Pruitt."

"I did not!" the judge cried.

Billy waved the Colt. "Both of you get over there by the stove."

They obeyed him.

Billy started backing for the rear door. "Now, big man, this is how it goes. I leave here, runnin'. You don't come after me 'cause you got the judge here. You can use Hizer's Remington. I'm bettin' you got so many fish to fry that you ain't gonna come after me."

Raider knew the Kid was right. He couldn't waste time chasing after him, not as long as he had the judge's sins to sort out. He had to admit the Kid had a few smarts.

Billy smiled and gave it one last wave. "So long, partner. If I don't see you again, don't fret. We'll see each other in Hell."

He ducked down the back steps and ran off into the night.

"Look it there, Judge," Raider said. "We both done let Billy the Kid get away. What d'you have t' say 'bout that?"

Ellrod fumed, not sure what to do next.

Raider reached for Murph Hizer's .44. "Don't get any ideas, Ellrod. You got some explainin' t' do."

As he lifted the Remington, Mrs. Pruitt eased into the kitchen. "Judge, I heard shooting. What . . ." She gawked at the dead man.

Raider eyed the judge. "She part o' this, Ellrod?"

He shook his head. "No. Let her be. Thelma, you go back upstairs. I'll take care of this."

She hesitated but then went out again.

"We'll have to get someone to stay with her," Ellrod said.

Raider ignored the comment. "Tell me, Judge. How'd you like t' go see Norris Hand? Huh?"

"I wouldn't like that very much."

Raider smirked. "Hand wasn't in on it, was he?"

"No."

"You set up the Kid without Hand knowin'. *You* killed Pruitt."

Ellrod lowered his head. "No. That was an accident. I made the mistake of talking to my old friend about my idea for a . . ."

"A gang?"

The judge nodded sadly. "A squad of men that would secretly do my bidding. It takes all of my salary to pay them, but I don't mind. Jack Pruitt and I had several cases in the Rangers that left us both well off. Gold that found its way into our coffers, gold that nobody missed if it was never found."

"Don't tell me," the big man rejoined, "that's how you kept 'im quiet. If he told anyone about your little vigilante operation, you'd turn him in for the gold he kept."

Ellrod sighed, shaking his head. "You show so much promise, Raider. If only you'd come to work for me."

"You still ain't told me why Pruitt was killed."

"I told you I didn't kill him!" He seemed to deflate, all the life running out of him. "That was Hizer. Somehow Jack figured out what I was doing. He was on the Flats one day when Hizer rode up on him. That sorry outlaw killed the best friend I ever had."

"You think Pruitt was goin' t' turn you in?"

Ellrod slumped back against the wall. "I know he was. He had written a letter. I found it in a secret place where he hid things."

Raider grunted disgustedly. "So you made it look like the Kid had killed Pruitt. Dumped the body and tipped off the sheriff."

"The Kid was just dumb luck," Ellrod replied. "Only when Hand found him there, I thought it was best to play out the drama. After all, the sheriff was hot to avenge the death of his brother-in-law."

"And you figured it was easier to whip up a lynch mob than to let me present evidence on behalf of the Kid?"

Ellrod smiled weakly. "It almost worked, didn't it?"

"Come on," the big man said. "We gotta go find the sheriff. He's gotta listen t' this. Even though I'm bettin' he won't want t' hear it."

EIGHTEEN

Raider made Judge Ellrod drag the body of Murph Hizer into the backyard. When he stepped out into the hot night, Raider peered into the evening shadows. He asked Ellrod how many men he had in El Paso. The judge assured him that Hizer and Simpson had been his only two operatives in the area. Raider knew that to be a lie, as he had seen at least four men on Red Clay Flats.

"Lead the way," he told Ellrod. "If there's any shootin', you'll be the first one dropped."

With the Remington pointed at his back, Ellrod walked down the main street toward the jailhouse. Raider cursed the Kid for taking his Peacemaker, but Billy had been so damned fast that the big man almost couldn't hold it against him.

"That Kid sure had a couple of good moves, didn't he?"

The judge grunted sadly. "I should have recruited him. Damn that sheriff. If he had let Bonney go, I wouldn't be in this mess now."

"Somebody woulda caught you sooner or later, Judge. Take my word for it."

They stepped up in front of the sheriff's office. It was dim inside, lit by a lamp that was almost out of oil. Raider eased the door open and stared into the dark enclosure.

"Hand? You here?"

Nothing.

The lamp flickered and then died.

Raider started in with the judge in front of him.

He heard the creaking as the door to the cell room swung open.

"Hand?"

A shape stood in the door frame.

"Hand, it's me, the Pinkerton. You gotta listen t' me . . ."

The shape slumped forward, falling onto the floor.

Raider pushed the judge out of the way, kneeling over the body. "Hand? What the hell is wrong with you?"

Then he heard the click of a revolver and felt the cold iron on the back of his neck.

A man said, "Fire up that other lamp, Judge."

When the light glowed, Raider looked up at the man with the Colt in his hand. "Friend o' yours, Judge?"

Ellrod reached down to take Raider's weapon. "Allow me to introduce Charlie Peck. A man sympathetic to my cause."

Raider gestured to the dead body of Norris Hand. "There's a man who wasn't sympathetic at all."

Ellrod snorted. "Hand was a fool. I wouldn't have trusted him with my operation. Of course, he would still be alive if you hadn't stumbled into this mess, Raider. I would have hung the kid and everybody would've been happy. Even that loutish sheriff."

Raider shook his head. "I can't say I really disagree with what you're doin', Judge. But it can't go on. You can't have death-riders killin' ever' man that done wrong. There's laws for that kinda stuff."

"I am the law," Ellrod replied. "Throw in with us, Raider. You'd be a welcome addition."

"I can't do it, Judge."

"Then become a marshal. Bring them in legally for me to try."

Raider sighed. "I'd have to think on it some. I might become a marshal. If you'd promise t' give up your riders."

Charlie Peck, a rough-looking drifter, glared at Ellrod. "You want me to kill him, Judge?"

"No."

"Hell," Peck said, "he ain't one of us."

Ellrod gestured toward the cell room. "Give him some time to think it over. Lock him up."

Peck had a strange look in his eye. "Okay, but if you decide to kill him, I want the chance. I ain't never killed a Pinkerton before."

Raider almost said that Peck was right, he could never ride with such lowlifes. He could never serve a man like the judge, someone who thought he was above the law. Raider didn't always agree with the right way of doing things and sometimes he even strained the boundaries of the law. But he never killed a man in cold blood and he never went after a man who didn't deserve it.

But he didn't say anything. He needed time. Maybe he'd figure a way to get out and even the score. Hell, there was no telling how many men the judge had on his side. He had been stupid to walk into the jailhouse trap. If he got out alive, he intended to see that it didn't happen a second time.

Charlie Peck closed the cell door and locked it. "Saw you comin' all the way, Pinkerton. Spotted you at the house and then I ran here and came in the back way, through that hole you made to free the Kid."

"You're a real rounder, Charlie."

"Hand was already dead," the drifter said. "I fooled you though. Got the drop on a Pink."

Ellrod stepped in front of the door. "You have until morning, Raider. I'll give you until then to decide if you want to join us."

The big man's eyes narrowed. "An' if I don't?"

"Then you hang for killin' Sheriff Hand."

Raider came up against the bars, glaring out at the judge. "Will I get a fair trial? Or will the lynch mob get me?"

Ellrod just wheeled and walked out.

Charlie Peck gawked for a while, then he left too.

Raider sat back on the cot, the one he had used when he had been locked up before. He wondered if Wagner could come looking for him. Would Tillie try to find him? Probably not before morning.

Maybe, if he could get a message to them . . .

But what would Wagner be against Ellrod and his men? Raider couldn't remember if the man with the wire spectacles had ever fired a gun. Certainly he couldn't take on a man like Charlie Peck.

"Damn it all."

But Tillie might help. Yes! That was it. He could always depend on her to know what was going on. She would get word before morning that Raider was in jail. She had a way of finding out things. Maybe she'd try to slip in disguised as the Mexican girl.

But his hopes faded almost as quickly as they had risen. Less than an hour after the door had been closed on his cell,

Charlie Peck returned with Wagner and Tillie, leading them at gunpoint.

"Company, big man."

Peck threw them in and locked the door again.

Wagner glowered at his associate. "Raider, will you tell me what the devil is going on?"

He sighed. "All right, Wagner. But don't expect too much from me. I ain't sure I got it all straight myself."

He had it straighter than he figured. They sat up most of the night, discussing it. Raider laid it all out for both of them, never missing a beat. He told the story like it had happened to someone else.

Wagner shuddered. "I don't believe it. Ellrod and his death-riders were behind the whole thing?"

"Near as I can tell," the big man replied.

Tillie was crying softly. "Poor Norris and Dub. They weren't bad men."

Raider patted her shoulder. "No, they weren't."

Wagner still had trouble believing the whole thing. "Ellrod also stirred the populace to a lynching along with operating a secret law-enforcement ring?"

"If they lynched the Kid, then Ellrod was off the hook," Raider replied. "It didn't matter if I could prove Billy innocent."

"Where is he?" Tillie asked.

Raider hung his head. "He went home, Tillie. I'm sorry 'bout that."

She kept on crying.

Raider pulled her close to him. "I know just how you feel."

Wagner started to pace back and forth. "Damn it all, there must be some way out of this."

"We could always ride with Ellrod," Raider offered. "Pretend t' be in cahoots with 'im till we get a chance t' make a break."

Wagner could not see the logic in that. "He wouldn't trust both of us, Raider. He'd probably hold Tillie and me captive so he could manipulate you in the direction he's going."

"Prob'ly. But that might be our only way out, pardner."

"Raider, if we get out of this with our lives, I promise you will never work another day for the Pinkerton agency."

The big man pointed a finger at him. "I'll hold you to that promise, Wagner."

He sure as hell would.

At dawn, Raider snapped awake, reacting to the sound of a creaking door. Boots clomped on the floor of the office. He listened in the quiet, wondering if Charlie Peck had come back to kill them. It wouldn't be hard. Just stick the gun through the bars and shoot them like ducks on the water.

The door to the cell room swung open.

More boots on the wooden floor.

A shape moved in the first light, eerie and purple like a spectre.

Raider flinched when a match struck the wall.

A circle of orange light illuminated the man's face as he touched the fire to the end of a cigarette. "Hello, Raider. Looks like you got yourself in a hell of a fix."

"Billy!"

The Kid just stood there, smoking his cigarette.

"What the hell are you doin' here?" Raider asked.

Billy chortled. "Hell, I figured you'd be happy to see me."

Raider slid up to the cell door, extending his hand. "I am, old buddy. I surely am."

Billy didn't shake hands with him. "I came back to see Tillie."

She stirred when her name was mentioned. "Who is it? What's all the commotion about?"

Wagner was also moving on the floor. "Raider?"

"It's okay," the big man said. "Billy's come back t' free us."

The Kid was staring at Raider. "What makes you think I'm gonna free you, Pink?"

Raider shrugged. " 'Cause I know you didn't come back for Tillie."

The girl slapped Raider on the back. "You can't say that about me!"

"Hush up, woman," the Kid said. "He's right. I didn't really come back for you. Why did I come back, Pinkerton?"

Raider grinned at him. "This is your only chance t' nail a

lawman, Billy. You can help us sink Ellrod an' his death-gang."

Billy nodded appreciatively. "You know, big man, that was great the way you figured all that. Just from seein' red clay on that horse's hooves. Yep, you sure did right by that one."

"So you're gonna help us get Ellrod?"

The Kid sighed. "I reckon, Raider. But you got to promise me one thing. That you won't try to take me in after we're finished."

Raider assured him that he wouldn't. He had no truck with William Bonney. Hizer had killed Pruitt, Ellrod had confessed as much. As far as Raider and Wagner were concerned, Billy wasn't wanted for anything in Texas.

Billy squinted at them. "You know, big 'un, Ellrod is gearin' up for something'. He's got a half dozen men at the widow's house. I know. I was watchin' the place."

A coyote smile from the big Pinkerton. "You never was gonna run off and leave me. Were you, Billy?"

Bonney shrugged. "Don't get sentimental on me, partner. I come back to kill Ellrod. Pure and simple."

Wagner bristled. "He has to be taken alive, Bonney, if at all possible."

"Sure, old man. Whatever you say."

Wagner turned to Raider, but the big man avoided his eyes. "Raider?"

"No guarantees," the big man replied. "'Cept one. When all o' this is over, the Kid goes free."

Wagner was starting to get huffy.

Billy stared straight into his steely gaze. "I walk, old man. *Now*, if you don't give me your word you won't try to take me in."

"You have my word," Wagner said finally.

Bonney tossed Raider the keys to the cell. "I'll see you at the warehouse under Tillie's place."

The girl pressed her face against the bars. "Where are you goin', Kid?"

Billy looked back at her. "Well, I figure since there's no law in El Paso tonight, I might as well make a few stops before the stores open. I hear there's a good gunsmith in town."

"Thieving!" Wagner cried. "You're as bad as Ellrod."

The Kid just laughed and walked out into the purple light of daybreak.

Raider put the key in the lock and turned it.

Wagner started to say something, but the big man told him to shut up. It was his game now. And he was going to stop Ellrod any way he could.

NINETEEN

A dark cloud was blowing down from the north, smothering the bright rays of the morning sun. Raider, Wagner, and the Kid were lying on the roof of the printing shop, watching the widow Pruitt's house across the street. The clouds deepened the shadows around the front door, where a guard stood with a double-barreled scattergun.

Raider grimaced, shaking his head and sighing. "I don't know. It looks pretty close here. Only one guard in front, but I'm thinkin' Ellrod has prob'ly got a slew of 'em inside."

"Out back, too," the Kid said. "Four of 'em sleepin' in the stable."

Raider looked at Bonney. "You said he had half a dozen boys with 'im. Four in the stable, one at the door. One inside. Six."

The Kid nodded. "Yeah, that's right. Unless somebody showed while I was gettin' y'all out of jail."

Wagner was staring intently at the house. "Well, Ellrod doesn't know we've escaped yet. He didn't leave a guard at the jail, which means he feels more comfortable with all his men at the house. Still not good for us."

Billy spun the cylinder of a shiny new Peacemaker he had "borrowed" from the gunsmith's empty shop. "I say we move quick, before he finds out we're gone. Get 'em while this cloud is in the sky."

Wagner wasn't sure he agreed. "We could hide until night. Even if Ellrod knows we're gone, we could move easier in the dark. Or we could leave and go for help."

Raider nodded. "That makes sense."

Billy the Kid snorted and made a raspy sound. "Shit, y'all are a couple of Alabama chickens."

"Six to three," Raider said. "Not good odds, especially if the judge is able t' get the town behind 'im."

"Then we go in and grab the Judge!" Billy offered. "Two of us watch the outside while one goes in after Ellrod."

Raider shifted, keeping his eyes on the house. "That front guard wouldn't be so hard t' take out. An' Ellrod ain't expectin' us yet. If we could nab Ellrod, then it wouldn't matter 'bout the others. Unless they decided to come after us. Then . . ."

"Boom!" the Kid cried.

Raider glanced toward Bonney, whose childish face wore an expression of total glee. "What's on your mind, Billy?"

The Kid reached into his shirt and pulled out a stick of dynamite. "Red Thunder," he said with a grin. "That should even things up."

Raider sort of thought he liked the idea. "Could work."

Wagner frowned at both of them. "You're crazy."

Billy nodded back toward the street. "We better decide in a hurry. Look yonder."

Charlie Peck had come out of the front door. He spoke briefly to the sentry and then started off down the street. Heading for the jail, no doubt, to check on his prisoners, to give Raider the final ultimatum—join Ellrod and his men or die. Now there was one less man in the house.

"We have t' move," Raider said. "Billy!"

"I'll take care of Peck," the Kid rejoined. "You got a knife?"

Raider pulled the blade from his boot and handed it to the Kid. "Make sure it ain't too noisy."

Billy flashed his pearly teeth in a broad grin. "No sweat, big man. Just go on and do what you have to do."

"Billy!"

"Yeah?"

Raider glared at him. "No tricks. When you finish with Peck, swing back t' the other side o' the barnyard an' cover us."

"I hear you, Pink-man."

He crouched low, heading for the ladder as fast as he could.

Wagner shuddered. "I'm not sure of this, Raider. It seems like a half-cocked plan to me."

"Don't worry," Raider replied. "It's completely cocked."

"But . . ."

"Look alive, Wagner. We ain't got time t' fret. It's time t' move now. You gotta be part o' this thing, too. I need you."

Sweat had broken out on the bespectacled man's white forehead. "Raider, I don't think . . ."

Raider clapped him on the shoulder. "Good, don't need no thinkin' now. Listen up, this is what I want you t' do . . ."

Raider watched from the roof as Wagner approached the sentry in front of the widow Pruitt's door.

"Just make it work," he said under his breath.

Wagner trembled like a cottonwood leaf in a cyclone.

So far nothing had been heard from the Kid. Charlie Peck was probably lying in an alley with his throat cut. The Kid had been right about moving on Ellrod before he learned of their escape. Raider just hoped they could get out of it without Wagner losing his life.

"That's it, William. Go on. Talk t' him."

He could read Wagner's lips: "Good morning. I'm here to see Judge Ellrod. I'm Judge Fenton, from Austin. Is the judge in?"

Just like they rehearsed it.

The sentry shook his head. No, Judge Ellrod could not see anyone. Not even another judge.

"Come on, Willie-boy," Raider muttered.

Wagner's mouth moved: "You see, I've come to pay him back some money that I owe him." His hand went into his pocket, taking out the leather pouch which was actually filled with Wagner's own gold. "I must settle this debt immediately."

"Atta boy, Willie. Come on. Drop it now."

"Ooops, clumsy me," Wagner seemed to say.

He let the pouch fall from his fingers.

"Sorry."

Raider held his breath as the sentry bent over to pick up the pouch. "Now, Wagner. Get 'im!"

Wagner pulled the horseshoe from inside his coat. He lifted it high overhead and brought it down on the man's skull. The sentry fell into the dirt, unconscious. Wagner started to drag him toward the alley.

Raider clapped his hands together. "Round one, Willie-boy. Now we gotta toe the mark for the next one."

He swung his legs over the parapet, hanging for a moment, dropping to the street, drawing his Peacemaker.

Wagner was coming out of the alley as Raider approached him. He held the sentry's scattergun in hand. His face was flushed red.

"Kinda gets your blood goin', don't it?" Raider offered.

"What do you want me to do?" Wagner asked.

"Just stand guard, pretend you're the sentry."

Wagner's lips trembled. "Raider . . ."

"Just do it. An' back me up if you hear any shootin'."

"Where are you going?"

The big man started for the front door. "Inside, old buddy. Inside."

"Hello, Charlie."

Peck turned to see Billy the Kid standing in the corner of the sheriff's office. "Billy?"

"Yeah, it's me. Charlie, you got to leave El Paso."

Peck grimaced. "Leave? I just got here."

"You got to leave," Billy insisted. "Don't ask me why. Just go and I won't do nothin' to you."

Peck squared his shoulders, dropping his hand next to the butt of his sidearm. "Kid, I can't do it. I can't."

"Okay, Charlie. But when you get to the other side, never say that I didn't give you a chance to leave peaceably."

Peck went for his gun.

Billy's hands moved a little quicker. Raider's knife flew through the air, lodging in Peck's throat. He lifted his pistol half out of the holster, but then fell to the floor, dying with noisy rasps.

Billy didn't even bother to pull the knife out. He just reached into his shirt and touched the stick of red dynamite. It was time to go and back up the Pinkerton. And maybe, to go kill a judge.

Raider eased through the front door, expecting to be fired upon at any moment. But the house seemed calm, almost cosy. The widow Pruitt was a fine housekeeper. Was she Ellrod's accomplice, though? The judge had said she wasn't in on it, but he might have been lying to protect her.

It was absolutely quiet as Raider hesitated in the dim light. He closed the door silently. Something clanked in the kitchen. Raider froze, listening. Another rattle that sounded like a metal pot.

Moving slowly, he made his way to the archway of the kitchen. He heard feet on the floor. His hand gripped the redwood butt of the Peacemaker. He thumbed back the hammer and held the weapon on the grey-haired man.

Ellrod had his back to him, standing next to the stove. He was watching a coffee pot. No sleep that night for the judge. A worried man.

Raider stepped into the kitchen. "Mornin', Judge."

Ellrod turned, flashing those grey eyes. "Raider! How the hell . . ."

Raider waved the barrel of the .45. "Don't tarry, Judge. We're goin' t' Austin t' see somebody with the authority t' punish you."

Ellrod started to back away.

"I mean it, Judge."

Ellrod opened his mouth and screamed.

Raider started to grab him.

A shot rang out from upstairs. The warning shot, the big man thought. Now all of Ellrod's men would be moving.

"Wagner!" the big man cried.

Shouts from the barnyard.

How many of them were coming?

It finally didn't matter. The explosion from Billy's dynamite rocked the whole town. It knocked Raider and Ellrod to the floor. The next thing Raider knew, a man was standing over him with a gun.

"This the Pinkerton, Judge?"

Ellrod nodded as he got up off the floor. His man had been upstairs. Raider hadn't figured that.

"Kill him," Ellrod croaked. "Now, before he causes me any more trouble."

Raider's eyes bulged as the man thumbed back the hammer of a Buntline.

"With pleasure, Judge. So long, Pink."

Raider tried to move, but he knew he would not be quick enough.

A scattergun exploded.

The man standing over Raider flew across the room, slamming into the hot stove. He rolled off the stove, trying to scream. But there wasn't enough left of his torso for him to make a sound.

Wagner stood in the archway, holding the smoking shotgun.

"Both barrels," Raider said. "I'm impressed."

Wagner dropped the gun like it was a poisonous snake. "I've never killed a man in my life."

Raider started to get to his feet. "Saved my bacon, Wagner. That's a fine time t' kill your first man."

He reached out to help Ellrod, who wobbled on his feet.

"Come on, Judge. Time for us t' leave El Paso. That explosion's gonna have ever'body awake."

"Ellrod ain't goin' nowhere!"

The Kid had come up the back steps. He had the new Peacemaker in his hand. Raider wondered if he could draw on the Kid, if it came to that. Billy was mighty fast.

"Thanks, Billy," the big man said. "You helped us with that dynamite. Why don't you just be on your way? Forget about Ellrod."

"Yes," the Judge said, backing toward the archway. "Just forget about me. You don't have to kill me."

"Yes I do," Billy replied. "I got to kill me a judge. A crooked judge. Ain't nobody gonna miss you."

He raised the Colt.

Ellrod backed toward the parlor, his hands held high. "Don't, Kid. Please. I deserve a fair trial."

"Like the one you were gonna give me!" Billy cried.

Raider and Wagner stood there, watching.

"Are you going to let him do this?" Wagner cried.

Raider looked at his Colt on the floor, wondering if he could reach it before the Kid plugged Ellrod. "Billy, don't. He'll stand trial."

Billy thumbed the hammer of the Peacemaker. "I hearby find him guilty as charged. I sentence him to one bullet between the eyes."

Raider moved for his Colt. A gun went off before he could reach the weapon. It didn't sound like Billy's pistol.

Ellrod staggered forward, whining like a horse in pain. He

turned a couple of circles, reaching for his own back, crashing into the kitchen table. He held the edge of the table for a second, trying to regain his balance once more before he died.

The judge slammed to the floor, twitching until the life ran out of him.

Raider looked at Billy. "You didn't shoot him."

The Kid was frowning. "I know."

Wagner gaped at the dead men on the floor. "My God. Ellrod was shot in the back."

They all turned toward the parlor.

The widow Pruitt stood there in the shadows with a smoking pocket revolver in her delicate hand. "I shot him," she said. "He killed my Jack. I knew it all along."

Raider and Wagner moved in to take the gun from her.

Wagner embraced the widow, who began to cry. "It's all right, dear lady. It's over now."

Raider nodded. "I reckon it is. Hey, Kid, thanks for the . . ."

But Billy the Kid was no longer standing there. He had gone down the back steps, to the stable. Raider heard him as he rode off to the north. Gone for good, back to New Mexico. Probably for the best, the big man thought.

He turned back into the kitchen, thinking it was time to pick up the rest of the pieces, as well as the rest of the bodies.

TWENTY

A crowd gathered in front of the widow Pruitt's house. Raider had to go out and explain to them what had happened. He culled out the mayor and a few of the town's leading citizens, giving them the responsibility of cleaning up the mess and tending the widow. They seemed to enjoy their part, even if it was the worst duty a man could draw.

Billy's dynamite had left the barnyard covered with chunks of Ellrod's unsavory gang. The kitchen didn't look too good either. The judge and his man had left a thick coagulation of blood on the floor. Raider had to explain why the judge was shot in the back. He also contended that the widow could not be held accountable for the shooting. She was just protecting herself when she shot Ellrod.

Raider also explained to the mayor and his men about the deaths of Norris Hand and Deputy Bagget. He told them about Ellrod's death-riders. The mayor replied that there would be an election for sheriff as soon as it could be arranged. Raider said they would send for state marshals to make sure the elections were held fairly. The mayor said he agreed.

When things were as settled as they could get, Raider got Wagner and headed for the telegraph office. He had to kick the door open with his boot. Ellrod had the place locked up tight.

"You know how to work one of those message keys?" Raider asked.

Wagner nodded. "I'm a bit slow, but I think I can manage."

"See that you do. Better get off a message to Austin. Then see if you can raise the home office."

Wagner stiffened, as if he had just remembered his station. "I'm well aware of the procedure."

Raider shook his head, smirking. "After all we been through, you're gonna pull rank on me now?"

Wagner pointed a finger at him. "You know something, Raider. This whole affair was almost botched by your impetuous nature."

"Almost only counts when you're playin' horseshoes, Wagner."

The little man threw out his hands. "And what will I tell Pinkerton? That we killed a judge?"

"We didn't exactly kill 'im, Boss."

Wagner snorted. "What about Hand and Bagget?"

Raider shrugged. "I'd say the widow Pruitt avenged their deaths."

"And the burial ground at Red Clay Flats?"

"Leave 'em lie, Wagner. It won't do no good t' go out there an' dig 'em up. Hell, I bet the great state of Texas wouldn't do it even if you told 'em 'bout the whole thing. They'll probably want t' keep it quiet."

Wagner exhaled disgustedly. "I suppose I better get started. Damn you, Raider. I'm going to have to skirt around the truth in this matter. I'll be surprised if Pinkerton lets us keep our jobs."

Raider started out into the street. "Well, let me know what happens."

"Where are you going?" Wagner cried.

But the big man did not look back, he just kept striding away from the little man in the wire-rimmed glasses.

When Raider returned at noon, he had Tillie with him. She had cooked a big lunch for Wagner, who rested in the telegraph operator's chair. Somehow Wagner seemed deflated, like the gunplay had taken everything out of him.

He opened his eyes when they came in. "Raider, where did you . . . oh, hello, Tillie. You're faring well, I trust."

She shrugged. "Well, the Kid left without sayin' good-bye to me."

Wagner smiled. "He wasn't the type of man you wanted to be with, Tillie. A scoundrel if ever there was one."

Raider waved him off. Women didn't like to hear you put down their boyfriends, even if they didn't love them too much anymore. Females were a lot more tender when it came to love, at least when their hearts were broken.

As Wagner started to eat, Raider noticed the pile of papers next to the telegraph key. "Any word from home?"

Wagner nodded. "The marshals will be here from Austin as soon as possible. I couldn't explain everything to them over the wire, but I managed to get the gist across. I daresay they won't believe it anyway."

"Probably right 'bout that," replied the rough-hewn agent from Arkansas. "Anythin' else?"

Wagner wiped his mouth with a napkin. "Well," he said, smiling, "the mayor has asked if you would like to run for sheriff, Raider. He seems to think you'd make a good one."

The big man shifted nervously. "Wagner, you know I couldn't do that. Now tell me if you've heard from the main office in Chicago."

Wagner nodded. "Fair enough."

"Am I still a Pinkerton?"

"You're still on probation," Wagner replied. "But that business in Tucson has been cleared up."

"You're kiddin'?"

"No." Wagner handed him the message. "Seems our man Stokes was able to get in touch with that Mexican sergeant you did business with. The man corroborates your story. The evidence was presented to a judge in Tucson and he ruled you were in the clear."

Raider hugged Tillie. "Glory be! I'm a Pink again."

"Maybe," Wagner said.

Raider's black eyes narrowed. "What you mean by that?"

"Just this," Wagner replied. "I have to go back to Chicago and convince Allan Pinkerton that you should stay on in our employ. I have to smooth everything out so Pinkerton doesn't fire you."

"And you'll do that?" the big man asked skeptically.

Wagner leaned back in the chair. "It would be easier if you came along with me."

"Ooh," Tillie said. "Can I go?"

Raider ignored her. "I ain't goin' back t' Chicago, Wagner. If you want t' plead my case for me, that's fine. But I ain't got nothin' t' be 'shamed of. I handle things my way. Y'all know that. You let me work alone for that very reason. Ain't no sense in changin' it now."

Wagner scowled at the big man. "If your job means anything to you at all, you'll come back to Chicago with me, Raider."

"My job means everythin' t' me, Wagner. I learned that the hard way. I ain't one for makin' any kind o' livin' but a honest one. I work my ass off for you and that Scotsman. You oughta know that. Hell, this wasn't even a real case. Nobody hired us. But I wanted t' do the right thing, and so did you as far as that goes."

Wagner fidgeted impatiently. "Then why do you refuse to come back to Chicago with me?"

Raider tipped back his Stetson. "'Cause I ain't kissin' anybody's ass t' keep this job. You got that? Nobody's. Not even Allan Pinkerton."

"You won't have to . . ."

"Yes I will. I'll have t' stand there on the carpet while y'all tell me what a disgrace I am. How I'm always fuckin' up. How I ain't the kinda man you want representin' your agency. Then you'll turn right 'round an' give me some chicken pickin' job that nobody wants. Ain't that right?"

Tillie touched Raider's arm. "Hey, honey, that ain't no way to talk to your boss."

"Shut up, Tillie, this is between me an' Wagner."

The little man's eyes were bulging. "You insolent bastard!"

Raider wasn't sure what "insolent" meant, but he didn't care. "You went through this thing with me, Wagner. And that oughta make us closer. You oughta see I don't always have it easy. But I jump right in. I ain't 'fraid t' be in the thick o' things. As far as I see, you ain't neither. You turned out t' be a brave man. Saved my life. Didn't back off once when your ass was to the wall."

"What's your point?" Wagner asked angrily.

"Just this." Raider took a deep breath. "I'm a gambler, you know that. An' now that you been in with me, you know 'bout takin' chances. I'm gonna take a chance here. I'm gamblin' that you're goin' back t' Chicago t' fight for me. I'll give you a month before I start t' look for work. If I ain't heard from you by them, too bad. But if you want me t' stay on, I'm willin' t' work for you."

"Is that it?"

Raider nodded. "Yep, I reckon it is."

Wagner stood up. "Now you better listen to me!"

Raider put his arm around Tillie, guiding her to the door. "So long, Wagner. I'll be at Tillie's for a while. Let me know if you need me for anythin'."

"Raider! You better come back here! I mean it! I'll get you fired in a second! Raider!"

But the big man only walked down the street, never turning back to Wagner, oblivious to his supervisor's strident threats.

EPILOGUE

Tillie came running up the stairs in a dither. She had something in her hand, a letter from the post office.

"It's from Chicago!" she cried. "From William!"

Raider was lying back on the bed, drinking from a bottle of whiskey. Wagner had only been gone two weeks. Maybe he had called Raider's bluff. Maybe the big man was fired after all.

"Aren't you gonna open it?" Tillie asked.

Raider shrugged. "You go ahead. See what it says."

Tillie tore open the letter and started to read.

"Yippee!" she cried. "William says Pinkerton wanted to fire you but he talked him out of it."

Raider chortled cynically. "I bet they got some kinda job that nobody else wants. Does it say anything 'bout an assignment?"

"No. Just that you're supposed to wait here until they get something for you. Hey, that sounds like you came out on top."

"Say anything 'bout pay?"

She read on, shaking her head. "No. But if you want to draw an advance on your salary, they will do it."

Raider had about fifty dollars left to his name. He figured it would be enough. Money never had meant much to the big man.

"Goodness," Tillie said.

"What?"

She looked up, her face glowing. "Says you've been given a commendation by the state of Texas for uncoverin' the thing with Judge Ellrod."

Raider grunted. "Commendation ain't much but a piece o' paper. I got 'em before."

"Oh, pooh."

She fell on the bed, hugging and kissing him. One thing led to another and they took off their clothes. Raider gave he a good ride, collapsing into her chest when he had finished They lay side by side in the afternoon heat.

"How you feelin'?" Raider asked.

Tillie sighed. "Okay. I reckon I'm over the Kid. It's bee easier havin' you here. I don't love you, Raider, but I . . ."

He put a finger to her lips. "Shh. I don't care if you don' love me. It's better that way."

They were quiet for a while.

Finally Raider kissed her on the cheek. "Hey, what say w get gussied up an' hit the town. Go out to that fancy restauran you're always talkin' 'bout."

She smiled at him. "You mean it?"

"Sure, honey. I still got that suit you gave me. And you'r a seamstress. You should be able to whip up somethin' prett for yourself."

She sat up. "Ooh, I got just the thing. But I'll have to was my hair. And you'll have to shave."

He kissed her breasts. "Yeah, we can share the tub down stairs."

Her hand went to his crotch. "I bet we can."

Raider was cutting into a fine steak, lopping off a bi chunk of meat. He pushed potatoes and onions onto the for and put the whole lump in his mouth. Tillie frowned at hi from the other side of the table.

"Raider! This is the nicest place in El Paso. Try to act lik a human bein'. You're eatin' like an Injun."

He wiped his mouth with a napkin. "Sorry, honey. I'm jus so hungry. You like to wore me out in that bathtub."

"Raider!"

He grinned at her. She had to smile back. She was having good time, despite his questionable manners. Everyone wa staring at them. A tall, black-eyed, handsome man and beautiful woman. The whole town knew about Raider's ex ploits, so they were sort of famous.

"Wait till I get you home."

Raider smiled. "Be good to me, darlin'."

They were finishing their meal when the commotion bega

on the other side of the restaurant. A man was trying to get past the hostess. He was pointing at Raider and saying something the big man could not make out. Raider started to reach for the derringer inside his coat, but then he saw that the man was wearing a tin sheriff's star. Raider waved to the hostess and nodded. She let them man pass.

The man with the star came toward them. He was clean-looking, neat, serious-faced. He had a pad and a pencil in hand.

Raider stood up, shaking hands with him. "I'm takin' you t' be the new sheriff, sir."

The man shook his head. "No. I'm not, at least not of El Paso. I've come about William Bonney."

Tillie put a hand to her throat. "Billy! Has something happened to him?"

"No," the man replied. "I just want to ask Raider a few questions. I understand from the marshal that you were in contact with Bonney."

Raider asked Tillie if she would leave them alone. Reluctantly she vacated her chair, glaring at the sheriff the whole time. Raider told her he would meet her back at her place. The man sat down in her chair. Raider joined him.

"Name's Garrett," the man said. "Pat Garrett."

"And you're lookin' for Bonney?"

Garrett nodded. "I have just begun. He's caused way too much trouble in New Mexico. It's time somebody did somethin' about it."

Raider leaned back in his chair. "Maybe. Although Bonney was okay to me. Didn't seem like that bad of a boy. I buried worse myself."

Garrett frowned. "I can tell you a lot about Bonney if you're willin' to listen. And then maybe you can tell me what you know about him."

Raider sighed. "Sheriff, I'm afraid you rode a long way for nothin'."

Garrett's eyes narrowed. "What are you saying?"

"That I can't tell you nothin' 'bout the Kid."

"But you were with him," Garrett insisted. "Didn't he say where he would be going next?"

Raider shook his head. "No. And I didn't ask 'im."

Garrett leaned over the table. "Don't let his face fool you, sir. Bonney is a hardened criminal, despite his youth. He's killed plenty of men."

"Of that, sir, I have not doubt," Raider replied. "But I can't talk 'gainst 'im."

"Why not?"

Raider got up from the table. "He saved my life, Garrett. A couple o' times. I just can't go 'gainst 'im, no matter what he done."

He started away.

"But you must!" Garrett cried. "You have to tell me!"

Raider never looked back.

When he walked into Tillie's, the girl was crying.

"Hey, honey," he said, stroking her shoulder. "Don't worry. Billy's safe. At least for now. I didn't tell that man a dad-blamed thing."

She looked up, her eyes red and teary. "You didn't?"

"No. Billy saved my life. That counts for somethin', don't it?"

She nodded.

"Hey," the big man offered, "let's fill that tub downstairs and go take a bath. It's still hot and I'm sweatin' under this monkey suit."

"Okay."

They went into the warehouse below, disrobing after they had filled the tub. Raider enjoyed the coolness as he settled in. Tillie slid in beside him, her body soft and curvy.

"Ain't that better, Tillie?"

"Look," she said. "It's floatin'."

She was pointing toward his crotch.

Raider kissed her full on the mouth.

Tillie laughed and grabbed his cock.

They splashed in the water for a long time, never once mentioning the kid named William Bonney.